T0131704

The
Tattered Collar

The Tattered Collar

Bob Arnone

iUniverse®

THE TATTERED COLLAR

Copyright © 2019 Bob Arnone.

All rights reserved. No part of this book may be used or reproduced by any means, graphic, electronic, or mechanical, including photocopying, recording, taping or by any information storage retrieval system without the written permission of the author except in the case of brief quotations embodied in critical articles and reviews.

This is a work of fiction. All of the characters, names, incidents, organizations, and dialogue in this novel are either the products of the author's imagination or are used fictitiously.

iUniverse books may be ordered through booksellers or by contacting:

iUniverse
1663 Liberty Drive
Bloomington, IN 47403
www.iuniverse.com
1-800-Authors (1-800-288-4677)

Because of the dynamic nature of the Internet, any web addresses or links contained in this book may have changed since publication and may no longer be valid. The views expressed in this work are solely those of the author and do not necessarily reflect the views of the publisher, and the publisher hereby disclaims any responsibility for them.

Any people depicted in stock imagery provided by Getty Images are models, and such images are being used for illustrative purposes only.
Certain stock imagery © Getty Images.

ISBN: 978-1-5320-7721-0 (sc)
ISBN: 978-1-5320-7722-7 (e)

Library of Congress Control Number: 2019910880

Print information available on the last page.

iUniverse rev. date: 08/01/2019

Dedication

To my devoted wife Pat, who spent countless hours in the process.
To our children and grandchildren, the blessing of our lives.

Chapter 1

In the Beginning

"**P**UT THE GUN DOWN, Mr. Peters, don't be foolish," said the priest, his tone calm and deliberate.

The distraught husband stepped closer to his intended target and shouted, "You think I'm being foolish? You're supposed to be a man of God and you're screwing my wife!"

"May I call you, Harry?" asked the thirty-year-old priest.

Peters didn't respond; his eyes were filled with hate and revenge as he moved the gun to the temple of his intended kill.

"If you do this, you won't be able to live with yourself," pleaded the man in the tattered collar, his expression, one of concern … as life quivered before him.

"Father, I hope … that God … forgives us both." The gun exploded with a thunderous echo within the hallowed grounds of the church.

Billy John Pratt had an unremarkable childhood until he reached his twelfth birthday. By the age of thirty-five, he had killed twelve people. He didn't have siblings and was an average student who never excelled in sports, music or the arts. The first encounter with his own sexuality occurred when he attended a party at a friend's house, chaperoned by the friend's twenty-one-year-old brother.

"Where's the bathroom?" asked twelve-year-old Billy. Someone pointed to the hallway. Walking in the corridor, he heard noises from the master bedroom. The door was slightly ajar, enough that he could see his friend's brother on his knees, caressing and kissing a female companion. Billy thought the ritual was disgusting, but as he turned away, an arm reached from behind the door, grabbing the back of his neck.

"Don't be afraid. It's Billy, right?" said Tim Walker, his friend's brother.

"I'm not afraid," Billy responded, feeling anxious but whispering bravado to his untested resolve.

"Then come with me, I have something to show you. Have you ever seen a naked woman?"

"N-no … n-no! … I haven't," stuttered the young boy.

"Isn't Emma beautiful?" asked Tim.

"Y-yes … yes she is," responded Billy.

"Would you like to touch her?"

The boy looked at the naked woman and lowered his head, not answering the question. Tim reached for the newbie's arm, reassuring him of the pleasure he was about to experience. Billy's hand was rigid and sweaty.

"Lighten up; she's not going to bite you," Tim said and then rubbed Billy's hand on Emma's leg. "Doesn't that feel good, Billy?"

"Y-yes, yes, it does," he nervously stammered, while beads of sweat formed on his brow.

As Billy continued to explore Emma's body, his heart beat faster, his hand reaching the softness of her inner thigh. The very thing he found loathsome a moment earlier was now the most pleasurable experience of his life—he didn't realize he was being molested by the two adults.

"I want you to feel what I do, Billy," said Emma, "when Tim kisses me where I'm going to kiss you." She began raping the minor without the thought of consequences.

Billy felt lightheaded and nauseated, so he ran to the bathroom, where he retched and prayed to the porcelain god.

He never saw Tim or Emma again, but they left their mark, shaping the destiny of a future killer. As a young teen and in the following years, Billy experimented with both genders and questioned his sexuality, often to the point of despair. Confusion was the rule during his senior year at Holy Cross College. He majored in English but was clueless about his future after graduation.

"Gregg, what are you going to do when you leave Holy Cross?" Billy asked his friend.

"I honestly don't know," said the twenty year old.

"The college is having a vocation day next week. Why don't you browse around? Maybe you'll click with something you see."

"Are you going, Gregg?"

"I wasn't, but I'll keep you company if you want to go."

"Yes, I'd like that," Billy responded.

Billy and Gregg were walking down the aisles, occasionally stopping at a kiosk to look at a brochure or talk to a company pitchman. Nothing seemed to interest Billy, and he concluded the experience was a complete waste of time. He started to exit the gymnasium when he heard someone call his name. He looked around, thinking it was Gregg, who had stopped to talk to a representative from a computer company, but it was Father Douglas, his parish priest.

"Hello, Billy. How are you?" asked the cleric.

"Bored to death, and before your recruitment speech, nobody's interested in the priesthood these days. Just the thought of celibacy would chase anyone away, Father."

"You're probably right, Billy."

"Father, can I ask you a personal question?"

"Fire away, Billy."

"Don't you ever miss sex?"

"Billy, did you ever take a cookie from the jar when your mother said no?"

"Of course, Father. Doesn't everyone?"

"Exactly my point, Billy."

Billy was astounded by the priest's honesty and continued to talk to him until the end of the evening. He was convinced what Father Douglas had proposed was a good idea. The priest, complicit in the embryonic growth of a sexual predator.

"Try the seminary," said Father Douglas. "Your master's degree will be paid for, as well as two years of free boarding. It'll give you time to evaluate your options. You don't have to take your final vows for two years, and who knows? Maybe it's your calling."

The idea intrigued Billy. It was a safe play, and he had nothing to lose.

The two years he spent in the seminary satisfied all of his expectations. He had the safety of community and found more than one who dipped into the cookie jar. His journey as a rapist and killer was about to begin.

After taking his final vows, Father Billy John Pratt was assigned to Saint Killian's Church in Boston, Massachusetts. His immediate supervisor was

Monsignor Gaston, who was seventy three and two years from retirement. There were two other priests in the modest parish, both in their early fifties, making Billy the youngest of the three.

The masses conducted by the young priest were well attended. His boyish looks and his humor during his homily attracted many of the young parishioners. His sermons were on the practicalities faced by those attending his mass; he avoided traditional preaching by the other priests. He even broke custom by having a ten-minute question and answer period for those in attendance; he did not ingratiate himself with the senior prelate of the church.

"Father Pratt, I'm puzzled as to why you interrupt the holy mass by allowing those in attendance to ask questions when they should be celebrating with prayer and reflection."

"Monsignor, don't you remember attending church on Sunday as a boy and counting the moments until the last blessing ended the mass? I want our parishioners to ask the questions they hide in their hearts. It gives them clarity instead of speculation or a misunderstanding of church doctrine."

"Father Pratt, the questions they ask can easily be answered by attending a catechism class here at Saint Killian's and not during the sanctity of the holy mass."

"Monsignor, with all due respect, that's not practical. These people have jobs and family responsibilities. They don't have time for what you're suggesting," the young priest said.

The monsignor was not pleased with such a brash response. "As the prelate of Saint Killian's, I'm demanding that you stop your question-and-answer time during mass. Do I make myself clear, Father Pratt?"

"As you wish, Monsignor, but I'm somewhat confused. My mass has the highest attendance, and you want to alter that success by changing something that's not broken?"

"Father Pratt, you seem to have a very high opinion of yourself. I suggest you pray to the Holy Mother Mary, asking for humility and obedience as a priest."

"I just don't get it, Monsignor. I provide a spark of curiosity in my mass by allowing our faithful to ask questions, and I'm chastised as being disobedient and lacking in humility."

So began the wide chasm between the monsignor and Father Billy John Pratt. The priest obeyed the senior prelate, but it left a bitter taste and was not the end of their conflicts. Billy's unbridled personality and youthful thinking was repressed by a man who had been a priest for almost fifty years. They were from two different generations, one conforming to the ways of the past, and the other, too progressive for the slow-turning machinery of ecclesiastical change.

Rather than resist the demands of the monsignor, Billy resolved to follow his initial plan of using the confessional as his hunting ground … and so it began.

"Bless me, Father, for I have sinned. It's been ten years since my last confession. Father, I don't know where to begin; it's been so long," said the person seeking absolution.

"Would you like my assistance?" asked the cleric.

"Yes, Father."

"Let's start with the Ten Commandments. Have you violated any of them?"

"Yes, I have, Father. I don't attend mass every Sunday. I've used the Lord's name in vain."

When she hesitated, the priest sensed her reluctance. He questioned her further and found that she had been unfaithful to her husband. Father Billy John Pratt had a potential victim to satisfy his excessive indulgence in sensual pleasures, but he wasn't ready to strike.

"Why do you think you've been avoiding the church?" asked the predator-priest.

"I guess … I got so busy in my life, and it just … kind of happened," she said nervously.

"What brought you here after ten years?"

"I don't know where to start, Father."

"The beginning is usually the best."

"Most people talk about men who have a midlife crisis when they turn forty. People don't think it can happen to a woman."

"Is that what's happening to you?"

"Yes, Father."

"Explain what you're feeling."

"I'm tired, Father. It's the same thing, day after day. I wake up, make breakfast for the children, go to work, come home, wash clothes, prepare dinner, and then am expected to be a teacher to the kids and a lover to my husband. The next day, it starts over again. I can't do it anymore," she said, her emotions spilling over.

"Don't cry, my child. You're not alone. I've heard the same frustration from several parishioners."

"That may be, Father, but it doesn't solve my problem."

She provided the opening for the predator. He asked her name—certainly a violation of anonymity in a confessional, but without hesitation, she told him.

The priest plotted a direction for the troubled confessor. "Mary, you seem lost and confused. It appears you expect an immediate solution to your problem. The answer from the church won't take away the pain you're experiencing."

"What can I do in the meantime? And no disrespect, Father, but please don't tell me to pray. That's not going to cut it."

It was time for the priest to act as the confessor tripped on the path he had devised. He didn't ask about her confessed affair; he wanted to avoid any suspicion of his intentions. She was unaware that her fate had been sealed.

"Prayer will go only so far, Mary. What you need is someone to talk out the problem, and it can't be done in a confessional."

"What are you saying, Father?"

"There are special situations when I meet with parishioners away from the church to discuss their concerns. It gives them a sense of privacy, not having to look over their shoulders at the blessed statues and the cross."

"I'd like that, Father. Can you come to my home?"

"Mary, if we're to talk, do you think meeting at your residence is a good idea?"

"My husband is on the night shift this week, and the children are in bed and asleep by nine."

"What does your husband do?" he asked, spinning his web.

"He works for the Transit Authority."

"When would you like me to come, Mary?"

"Tonight would be convenient—if you're available, that is."

"Where do you live?"

"I'm only four blocks from the church, 345 Bailey Street. Is nine o'clock good for you, Father Pratt? The name on the mailbox is Peters. Ring once, and I'll buzz you in."

"If I'm not there by 9:30, an emergency came about. Leave me your home number before you leave," said the priest.

"Father, would you like me to save some supper for you?"

"No, thank you, Mary. Make a good act of contrition, and for your penance, say ten Our Fathers and ten Hail Marys."

"Father Pratt, the building fund committee is meeting tonight at eight o'clock. I was to attend the meeting, but my sister took ill and I have to shoot over to the Catholic Medical Center. Can you make it in my place?" Asked Monsignor Gaston, St. Killian's pastoral leader.

"I have an evening call, Monsignor. Can you have Father Ralph or Father Simon attend?"

"You know, Father Pratt, house visitations are not recommended. Are you sure it's necessary and what's the intended good?"

"Monsignor, when I was assigned to the parish, the first thing you said to me was—and I quote—'William, know the people.' I can only know them on their terms. If you wish me to cancel God's work, I will."

"Father Pratt, God's work is where I say it is. Do we understand each other?"

"Yes, Monsignor. Do I cancel this evening's appointment?"

"If either Father Ralph or Father Simon is available, keep your appointment. If neither is, I want you to attend."

The embattled priest resented the seventy-three-year-old senior leader but said, "By all means, Monsignor."

For his part, the monsignor was suspicious of this young upstart and his interactions with parishioners. "You know, Father Pratt, I retire in two years, and Saint Killian's will be looking for a new pastor, someone who's familiar with all aspects of the community."

"Monsignor, with all due respect to your position, you know the church would consider me too inexperienced to be selected as pastor, and I have no interest in becoming your successor. Others here are better suited." The young priest found it strange that the elder cleric would use his succession as bait, considering their differences.

"I find it rather unusual for a young priest to be devoid of ambition. Why is that so, Father Pratt?"

"I've never had the ambition to be a politician. I believe you lose touch with the people."

The comment angered the monsignor. "Father Pratt, are you hinting that I've lost touch with the people of Saint Killian's?" the prelate snapped.

"No, no, Monsignor, you have your parish priests to keep you informed about the people, and if I'm being perfectly honest, you and I know that your successor will be a seasoned priest," Pratt said. His unspoken message was clear—he could play the game of relational chess to near perfection.

"Father, I suggest you limit your sarcasm and choose your words carefully. If you're unhappy in your current assignment, I can always arrange for a transfer.

Maybe Boston isn't the conducive environment you seek. Perhaps a more secluded place in one of the church's desert enclaves would be more suitable for your needs."

"Monsignor Gaston, I go wherever the calling takes me. Whether it's here at Saint Killian's or some other parish is inconsequential to me."

Gaston despised Pratt's arrogance and felt there was something more than the generational difference between them. His subordinate was thirty years old and handsome—a slender one-hundred-seventy-two- pounds, six feet tall, with sandy-blond hair. He looked more like a movie star than a priest and didn't present himself as a conservative clergyman of the church. The women of the parish paid a lot of attention to Father Pratt. His charm and good looks overshadowed the white collar around his neck. Billy's masses were better attended than others, which drew criticism and envy from the other priests in the church. His sermons addressed the realities of the world, rather than the traditional hell and damnation preaching of the older priests.

But the monsignor was stuck; the shortage of priests meant the church was desperate. New priests were recruited from all over the world, but the lenient criteria was an insult to someone from the old guard like Gaston. It was a great clash of cultures that tested a priest's continued commitment to a life of service and abstinence.

The monsignor had a bad feeling about his young priest. He hoped to avoid a scandal in his parish before retirement. The church had had its share in recent years and in most situations, the blame was placed on the lead pastor. He would keep a special diary on the daily whereabouts of Father Pratt.

"May I go, Monsignor?" Billy asked.

"Father, I want you to provide me with a daily schedule of visitations outside of the church—who you're seeing and the nature of the visit," the Monsignor demanded.

"Why, Monsignor?"

"Because, Father Pratt, I command you to do so!"

"Will all parish priests be required to establish the same reporting schedule?" Billy asked.

"Yes, Father Pratt, they will."

"Good. For a moment I thought you were singling me out on a whim."

"Father Pratt, if I wished to single you out, it would be direct and with cause. The use of the term *whim* is more to the taste of your unbridled youth and certainly has no place in this conversation. Please give me your schedule for the remainder of the day." At this point, the monsignor's veins were protruding from his neck.

"Yes, I will, and I do hope that your sister gets well. I'll pray for her recovery," Billy said with a wry smile.

"Thank you, Father, and I will pray for yours."

Billy was ordained a priest when he was twenty six years old. He'd grown up in Pittsburgh and had attended Saint Cecelia High School. Upon graduating from Holy Cross College, he entered the seminary. Saint Killian's was his first assignment in Boston, and Monsignor Gaston would be the obstacle to his world of fantasy. He would have to endure the prelate for two more years. *Perhaps*, he thought, *it will be less.*

Chapter 2

Forgive Me, Father

AS FATHER PRATT WALKED to Mary Peters's apartment, the thought of his conversation with Monsignor Gaston brought a smile to his face. He climbed up the steps to the Bailey Street building and rang the bell but didn't wait for the buzzer—the door to the entrance was unlocked.

Across the way, eighty-four-year-old Connie O'Reilly was a curious observer from her second-floor window.

Billy knocked on apartment 2B, his thoughts illicit and calculating. The door opened, and there was Mary Peters, dressed like a person going on her first date. She was an attractive woman, standing five six and weighing one-hundred-thirty-three well proportioned pounds. Her shoulder-length silky brown hair glistened in the hallway light. Her perfume was distinct yet subtle. Mary wore a powder-blue blouse and a short tan skirt. Her high heels made her taller in appearance and showed off her strong and alluring legs. Billy was consumed and fascinated, fixed in place—until she spoke.

"Welcome, Father Pratt, I'm so glad you could make it," Mary said, her tone, upbeat and pleasing.

"Thank you, Mary, for having me in your home." The priest's eyes moved about the apartment as she ushered him inside.

"Please make yourself comfortable," said Mary.

Billy moved to the couch and sat down. The apartment was spacious—three bedrooms, a large kitchen, and a generous family room. The priest crossed his legs, his lips muttering what he had been trained to do—pray for restraint, try to overcome his carnal visions of Mary, and not succumb to his self-indulgent needs. His thoughts suddenly were interrupted.

"Can I offer you a drink, Father Pratt?" Mary asked, her lips sensuous and ripe.

"I'd love a drink, but please call me Billy." And so began the flirty and playful behavior.

"You want me to call you *Father* Billy?"

The girlish response amused the priest. "No, Mary, just Billy," he said.

Their eyes met, and the expectations of both rose to another level.

"Okay, Billy, what are you drinking?"

"Do you have scotch?"

"Yes, I do. Straight or with ice?"

"Ice dilutes the taste," said the priest.

Mary poured two scotches and then walked to the stereo and pushed the button to play an uninterrupted medley of love songs. She approached the couch and sat a pillow apart from the priest. Her loins anticipated past fantasies she'd had while listening to his sermons at Sunday mass.

The priest began by diverting the conversation from his ultimate intention. "So, Mary, how old are your sleeping youngsters?"

"Actually, Father—"

"*Billy*," he interrupted.

Mary placed her hand on his right shoulder. "Sorry, Billy."

The priest glanced at her hand, and the foreplay began.

"The children probably *are* sleeping, but they're staying at their aunt's tonight. I thought our discussion should be as private as possible." Their eyes met with eager anticipation of the events ahead. Mary's woman's intuition told her the priest would be a willing participant. "And they're six and seven."

"You started your family late."

"Harry and I didn't marry until I was thirty."

"How was life before, Harry?"

Mary sighed heavily. "I don't know where to start, Billy."

"That sounds like a familiar phrase. Why don't you start with your childhood? Where were you born?"

"Right here in Boston. I went through the public school system. I'm one of three children. My older sister and brother both live out of state. Nothing special about growing up; the same bumps and bruises as everyone else."

"Did you go to college?" he asked as his imagination gained traction.

"Boston University. I was a real hometown girl. I majored in sociology and then joined the Peace Corps after graduation."

Her answer surprised him. "Why the Peace Corps?"

"When I was growing up, I never once left Boston. It was an opportunity to see different countries. I guess being young and idealistic, I was going to help save the world. I was disillusioned when I was assigned to Cameroon on the west coast of Africa. I worked in a village just outside Yaounde, the capital."

Billy was fascinated as he listened to Mary's exploits, for he never had left the continental United States. She was very animated while explaining her two years in one of the poorest nations in the world. Every movement of her body generated another level of anticipation. He knew the final outcome would be an experience of pure pleasure, but he didn't want to be obvious. Perhaps he was reading the wrong signals from her, and his intentions would better be served by delaying them and scheduling another visit. With the monsignor's warning very clear, he wanted to avoid a clumsy misstep and receive a complaint from a parishioner. He would let Mary make the first aggressive advance.

"After Africa, then what?" he asked.

"I was twenty five and a little smarter. The next two years were in South Africa. The poverty was different, but my running was a lot more picturesque."

"Running?"

"Yes, Billy, running. It's my only passion in life. It started in college. I ran as a hobby. I continued to run in Africa—it gave me a sense of control."

"What kind of control, Mary?"

"I didn't require anyone to participate; it was just me and nature. It cleared my mind. I felt a freedom, an exhilaration within, without rules or limitations."

"I'm truly impressed, Mary. And where did you meet your husband?"

"He was a sociology major at Boston University. We dated for a while and then went our separate ways. When I joined the Peace Corps, he dropped out of college to get a job. He's been working for the Transit Authority ever since. When I left the Peace Corps, I came home to Boston. When you're growing up in a city, it seems like a country, until you see the rest of the world. One Friday night, a few of my friends and I went to a local club, and there was Harry. We dated again and married when we were both thirty. The rest is history."

"When did the problems begin?" Billy asked.

"It was good in the beginning. We started a family two years later—first

Robin and then Harry Jr. I guess we got into a rut when I turned thirty-eight and realized this was it, as good as it gets. Harry isn't athletic, and his horizons are limited. He can't see beyond Boston, his job, and bowling with the guys. Don't get me wrong; he's a nice guy, but that's it. We've drifted apart to the point that … I'm ashamed to say it … I sought sanctuary with another man. It was like running, I was free to let my feelings and inhibitions lead to a new place. I knew then that it was a matter of time before my marriage would fail."

"Have you addressed your feelings with your husband?"

"I've subtly approached the subject. And when I did, he'd come home with flowers, take me to dinner, and grunt his way to sleep. It worked for him, but it's been a nightmare for me. I feel trapped and don't like the thoughts swirling inside my head."

"What kind of thoughts, Mary?" The priest was laying the foundation for him to be the answer to her prayers.

"You don't want to know, Billy."

"How can I help if you don't share your feelings with me?"

"I'm embarrassed, Billy."

"Mary, as a priest, I've heard just about all of it and then some. Nothing surprises me anymore."

"Billy, how old are you?"

"Thirty, this past week. Why do you ask?"

"Here I am, a forty-year-old woman, asking a thirty year old for advice."

"I consider age just a number, and is it advice you're looking for, Mary, or something else? Share your thoughts with me."

"My thoughts could damn us both and lead us to nothing but trouble."

The priest had his opening. She had raised the curtain, and it was now for him to accept her offering. It would be calculated and swift. He rose from the couch and placed his drink on the coffee table. "I see that I'm wasting my time here, Mary."

When he started toward the door, Mary reached for his hand. "Please don't leave, Billy." The pain of her soul bled the tears from her eyes, the shame in her lust for the handsome priest, unlocked.

He took hold of Mary's hand and pulled her up from the couch. He put both arms around her waist and kissed her passionately.

Mary surrendered to her craving, opening her mouth to accept his probing kiss. She took his hand and led him to her bedroom.

"Father Pratt, how was your visit yesterday evening?" asked Monsignor Gaston, shuffling papers on his desk.

"It went rather well, Monsignor. I was pleased with the results."

"What time did you return to the rectory?"

"Didn't Mrs. Owens tell you?"

"Father, Mrs. Owens retired at ten o'clock."

"Then, Monsignor, it must have been after ten," Billy said, with an ironic smile.

"Was the family problem so dire that your attention was required at such a late hour?"

"Both the parishioner and I considered the time, but our progress was too important to be interrupted by constraints. The decision garnered significant results."

The monsignor narrowed his eyes. "Will the problem require future nocturnal visits?"

"In fact, Monsignor, I believe it will require my personal attention with several follow-up discussions."

"What is the basis of the problem? Perhaps I can offer some guidance to the issues at hand."

"Thank you, Monsignor, but this is a situation that requires a one-on-one relationship, uninterrupted by a third person."

"Father Pratt, considering that you've been a priest for only four years, don't you think discussion from a more experienced individual would prove more productive? Is this parishioner male or female?"

"I thought the journal that you mandated would serve the same purpose as the questions you're asking," Billy said, trying to avoid the Monsignor's trap.

"You haven't fully answered my question. Is the parishioner a male or female?" When he observed Billy's hesitation, he became visibly annoyed; this young priest was testing his patience.

"The parishioner is a female, Monsignor."

"Bring your journal to me, Father Pratt."

The priest left the room, returning soon after with his journal in hand. He tossed it on the desk. "Here it is, Monsignor."

The monsignor scanned the entry and then read it aloud. "'Mary Peters, 345 Bailey Street … 9:00 P.M. to 10:45 P.M. Problem … parishioner questions faith.' This is the extent of your entry?"

"I wanted to be as brief as possible. You've stated several times that I should resolve to listen more and talk less. You've said that no one ever learns by talking."

"Mrs. Owens! Mrs. Owens!" the prelate called out and then heard her scurrying footsteps coming from the kitchen.

"Yes, Monsignor," she responded, gasping for air.

"Please make me a cup of tea," he said with obvious frustration.

"Yes, Monsignor. Would Father Pratt also like a cup of tea?"

"You know I hate tea, Mrs. Owens. I hear it sometimes disagrees with one's temperament," Billy sniped, feeling combative.

Mrs. Owens looked at the monsignor, surprised by the young priest's sarcasm.

"Don't just stand there, Mrs. Owens. I would like my tea by this afternoon," snapped the monsignor, waving her from the room. He returned his attention to Billy. "Do you intend to be unresponsive for the rest of my tenure here at Saint Killian's?"

"Can we be honest with one another, Monsignor?"

"Yes, Father Pratt, please do so."

"It seems obvious you don't like me, and quite frankly, I don't like you. Why create waves two years before you retire? I suggest we stay out of each other's way. It'll make both of our lives less stressful."

"You arrogant son of a bitch! The only reason you're still here is that the holy church is hard up for priests. In my day, you'd never leave the seminary!"

"*In your day*, Monsignor? Why do you think the church is in such disarray? Old thinking priests like you created the legacy we've inherited. You're a role model that discourages anyone from joining the seminary."

"Then why did you join, William?" the monsignor asked, suddenly becoming formal.

"When I was in college, there was a priest who whispered the right tune in my ear."

"Well, let me give you a tune of my own, Father Pratt. If you do anything to embarrass the church, I'll crucify you. And be on notice, I will take a closer look at your late-night visitations, which will include my personal contact with the parishioners. If I get a sense of impropriety, I'll not only suggest to Rome that you be defrocked, but I'll report you to the civilian authorities. In the meantime, while you remain under my guardianship at Saint Killian's, you will follow my instructions to the letter. If you can't, I suggest you contact the diocese and request a transfer. But be aware, sonny, that if you do, a personally drafted letter to the bishop will guarantee that your next assignment will be as a missionary in some remote part of the world. Is that honest enough for you, Father Pratt?"

"Perfectly, Monsignor Gaston, and I'll consider my options."

"You do so, because I see only two choices: be a good little boy, or quit the priesthood. Now get me a detailed summary of your meeting with Mrs. Peters by dinner, or I'll presume you've decided upon the second alternative."

"You'll have your report by supper, Monsignor. By the way … how is your sister doing?"

"It's a bit late to kiss ass, Father Pratt."

The young priest picked up a pencil from the monsignor's desk, snapped it in two, and then left the prelate's office.

The report was completed by the requested deadline, although scattered with lies and words that the monsignor wanted to hear. Billy called Mary Peters, warning her about the impending inquiry from his superior. She assured him that Gaston would receive a glowing and grateful response.

But deep within Billy's psyche, the monsignor was an obstacle to his purpose and had to be dealt with more forcefully.

The monsignor made good on his promise and called Mary Peters. He had lost his objectivity and was so infuriated with his young priest that he hoped to find that Billy had transgressed and conducted an inappropriate relationship with a parishioner.

Instead, Mary told him, "Monsignor, Father Pratt was a spiritual revelation. His personal attention to our problem was deeply appreciated and up-lifting. I'm sure his future guidance will help my family to resolve our issues. I wish the church had more young priests like Father Pratt. You should be very proud of him."

It wasn't what he wanted to hear, but he was relieved. A scandal under his leadership would have tarnished his years of devoted service.

"Thank you, Mrs. Peters. The church wants to make sure our parishioners are receiving the help they need. I would like to speak to your husband to hear his impressions of Father Pratt's spiritual guidance."

"He's at work, Monsignor, but I assure you that he'd give the same assurances about Father Pratt," said Mary, and then she thought, *What a persistent old goat.* She had a new inspiration in her life, and she wasn't going to allow anyone to ruin her newfound adventure.

"I can't believe that old bastard called you," Billy said when they next met. "The grapes on that guy! I would have given anything to see his face when you laid it on him."

"Are you grateful?"

"Yes, Mary, I am."

"Then show me how grateful," she said, her eyes sending a clear message.

The priest kissed Mary, first on the nape of her neck and then her ear, providing the sensual stimulus, and they retreated to the bedroom.

Mary's daily running had sculptured a figure that made her look ten years younger than her age. The young cleric undressed the sensuous woman until only her underwear remained. Billy took a step back and stared at her beautifully contoured body, while musing that the monsignor wasn't going to ruin it all.

"What's wrong, Billy?" Mary asked.

"Nothing. You're simply beautiful to look at, and I'm so grateful that you've become a part of my life."

He said the right things to his new conquest. But she didn't know the real man behind the cloth; he just happened to be there when she was looking for a new spark to solve her dilemma. She had fantasized about him during her self-indulgence, but she never imagined, not in her wildest expectations, that the priest would be the answer.

"You're making me blush," Mary whispered, reaching to remove the last of her underclothing and then extending her arms and commanding the priest embrace her. She surrendered, signaling her desire to become one with the fallen priest, as she quivered with each embedded movement.

At the conclusion of the tryst, both were lying in bed, gently whisking their hands back and forth on each other's naked body, each with thoughts that were similar in concern but dramatically apart in their conclusions. Mary's sentiments were about her husband and how she would ultimately address wanting to leave, while Billy was plotting the most egregious act.

"I believe Harry is beginning to suspect something is wrong," said Mary. Startled, Billy propped himself up. "Why do you say that?"

"He and I haven't been together since you and I met. I find it distasteful to surrender myself in a loveless marriage."

"Mary, do you want to destroy what we have?" Billy asked, now in a sitting position.

"No, Billy," she said, feeling some trepidation.

"Then you have to accommodate him," the priest demanded.

"I don't think I can, Billy. It wouldn't be real … and … I've fallen in love with you."

"As long as I'm a priest, this is all we have. We can't be seen in public. They are no dinners out or vacations to take. Think hard about this, Mary, because the bed we share is who we are in the foreseeable future. If you want me out of your life, I'll understand."

"No, Billy, please don't ever think about leaving me. Promise you won't; promise me." Mary embraced him, seeking reassurance.

"Then do as I ask. I need time, Mary. I have to figure out where I belong, and I won't have that answer in a day, week, or month. I ask for your patience and devotion."

"I'll do as you wish, Billy, but I'll be thinking of you when I'm with him." Feeling overwrought, she wrapped her arms around her lover as a tear trickled down her cheek.

The priest once again became aroused; his twisted thoughts of Mary and her husband's sexual activity were the catalyst, while observing through his own looking glass. They embraced, surrendering to their passion.

"Father Pratt, Monsignor Gaston is at his Monday meeting with the bishop and won't return until late this afternoon," said Mrs. Owens, the rectory caretaker. "Fathers Ralph and Simon accompanied the monsignor. I have some errands to do and will be back in about two hours. Is there anything you need before I leave, Father?"

The priest smiled. "Don't concern yourself. I'll be fine."

Billy knelt in a pew of the church, looking at the cross on the wall. He asked for forgiveness of his thoughts, past deeds, and the one he was about to commit. Somewhere in his demented mind, he asked God to absolve him while sanctioning his actions. He walked to the second floor and opened the door to the Monsignor's private sanctuary, a room dedicated to his meditation and access to parishioners with whom the monsignor would address weekly from the oval balcony. He did so every Tuesday at noon and would thank the parishioners for their devotion to the church. It was a brief acknowledgement, usually five minutes or less, but attended by long time members of the parish as a tradition and to receive the monsignor's special blessing.

It was the perfect opportunity for Billy to silence the cleric. He removed three of the four bolts at both ends of the balcony—those that secured the landing—and placed them in his pocket. The church was more than seventy-five years old and in need of several repairs. The collapse of the balcony would be a testament to the decaying structure.

The next morning, after the seven o'clock services, Gaston called his three priests to his office. He reviewed the bishop's guidelines regarding clergymen, commanding them to avoid off-church visitations to parishioners, particularly if a female member had made the request. The monsignor looked directly at Billy, who was convinced that he was Gaston's target.

Billy simply smiled and envisioned the cleric falling from the balcony to his death. When the meeting was over, Billy retreated to the confessional. There were ten parishioners waiting outside the church for the monsignor's blessing. It was 11:30 A.M.

"Bless me, Father, for I have sinned. It's been six months since my last confession. Father, I've disobeyed my parents on several occasions. I've had impure thoughts, and I've committed impure deeds," said a young confessor.

"How have you disobeyed your parents?" asked the priest.

"I'm gay, Father, and my parents have forbidden me to see my friend. I want to run away, but I'm afraid it'll expose my partner to his parents—they don't know."

"Are the impure deeds exclusive to your friend, or are there others?"

"Others?" The confessor was taken by surprise at the question.

"Yes, do you have relationships with other boys?" Pratt asked.

"I'm a member of a gay club that my friend and I formed in high school. We meet once a week at whoever's house is available, or we sometimes pool our money and rent a hotel room."

"Why do you consider your meetings as impure deeds?" Billy asked, looking at his watch.

"We play games, Father."

"What kind of games, my son?"

"Father, I'm embarrassed; perhaps I should go."

"No, don't leave. I'm here to help you, and that's why you're here. Let me be your friend. What's your first name?"

There was silence from the young confessor. He'd never been asked his name in a confessional and was taken aback. "It's … Christian, Father."

"I need your help, Christian. I can't be a good priest unless I can walk out from this confessional and feel like I've somehow helped you to resolve your problem. That's why I need you to help me to be a good priest. Will you help me, Christian?"

"I'll try, Father," he said, though the teenager was clearly confused.

"Good man, Christian. Now, help me to understand you and your friend."

"I love him, Father. I can't think of life without him. My world with Kevin is pure and uncomplicated."

"How did your parents find out about Kevin?"

"He was staying at my house for the weekend, and my sister asked my mother why Kevin was in our home. When my mother asked why she'd asked such a question, my sister told her that the whole school knew that Kevin was gay. I was guilty by association. My mother and father confronted me with the question about my sexuality, and I told them the truth. After that, they threatened to confront Kevin's parents unless I stopped seeing him."

"Do you think it would be better for both of you if Kevin let his parents know?" Billy sounded concerned, but his motive was self-serving.

"Father, you don't know Kevin's parents. They'd send him away to a private school. We'd never see each other again."

"You may be right, Christian. Perhaps telling his parents would be a mistake. You both will have to be very careful in the future. How old are you, Christian?" Billy looked at his watch once again.

"Sixteen."

"You seem like a bright young man. What do you do when you don't want your parents to know what you're doing?"

"I take away all suspicion and cover my tracks."

"Well, now, I think you just came up with a solution."

"You're a cool guy, Father. I like your style."

"Thank you, Christian. I think we can help one another if you're willing to try. Monsignor Gaston wants me to get more involved with the young people of the community. I need someone like you to … kind of show me the ropes, to get your friends to trust me enough to talk. Could you meet me one evening, perhaps in your home, so we can plan a good strategy?"

The teen hesitated, surprised at the request. "Why would you want to meet at my house?"

"Don't you want your parents to think you've found a better alternative than … Kevin. What better way of covering your tracks?"

"Very smart, Father. My friends are going to like you."

"I'm sure to like them too, Christian. What would be a good night for us to get together?"

"Can I call you, Father? I have to ask my parents first. I don't want you to just show up. My mother would have a heart attack."

"Sure, Christian. Make sure you give your address to Mrs. Owens when you call with the day and time."

"Mrs. Owens?"

"She's the rectory's secretary, cook, and general pain in the butt."

"I will, Father. By the way, my last name is DeVoe."

"Well, Christian DeVoe, say ten Our Fathers and ten Hail Marys and a good act of contrition."

The time was 11:55 A.M., and the next parishioner who entered the confessional was quite upset because of the time she had to wait.

"Bless me, Father, for I have sinned, and it has been three weeks since my last confession. I've used the Lord's name in vain several times, even while waiting for the young man in front of me to finally leave."

"I'm sorry for your wait. God doesn't place a time limit on a confessor."

"Does God allow a priest to fool around with a parishioner?" asked the crusty, Connie O'Reilly.

Billy was astonished and didn't respond. There was an eerie silence in the confessional until he finally asked the woman to clarify her comment.

"I have observed weekly visits by a priest, conveniently when the husband wasn't at home."

He had to defuse her observations by suggesting that her suspicions were unfounded. He knew she was referring to him and had to fill in some presuppositions to create doubt. "A person's distress, at times, requires tender understanding of the issues through one-to-one intervention," he said.

"Please, Father. *Tender understanding*, my foot. It doesn't require personal embraces, which I can clearly see through open window blinds."

"Those are serious allegations. Perhaps what you saw was a priest comforting a distraught parishioner. Who are you? Are you aware that your allegations can cause a serious problem for your church and your neighbor?"

"I know what I saw, and so will Monsignor Gaston. It's priests like you who should be thrown out of the ministry. Shame on you, Father."

"What's your name!" he demanded, not caring that the confessors waiting in line were getting an earful.

"I'm Mrs. O'Reilly, and—"

Before she could continue, a thunderous noise bellowed throughout the church.

Billy was stunned by the woman's menacing threats, giving him another obstacle to deal with, but now, he immediately ran toward the screams coming from the side entrance of the church. When he opened the door, he saw something he had not anticipated. He wanted only the monsignor dead, but in the rubble, lay the bodies of Father Ralph and Father Simon.

According to Mrs. Owens, they had joined the monsignor and were standing by his side when the balcony collapsed. Mrs. Owens turned toward Father Pratt and collapsed into his arms. All three of the prelates had lost their lives; the fall from the second floor and the falling debris had been a crushing blow. The parishioners below the collapsed balcony were unscathed but in shock, as they had witnessed seventy-five percent of their church leaders tragically taken. They, of course, were unaware that murder had been committed by the surviving priest of the parish.

A man of the cloth had crossed the line from debauchery to killer and showed no remorse. He was now unchained from the shackles placed upon him by Monsignor Gaston and was free to pursue whatever fed his hedonistic desires.

The next day, a detective from the local precinct visited the scene. He asked Father Pratt if he could see Monsignor Gaston's office. The unholy priest directed Mrs. Owens to escort him to the room.

The detective leaned over the opening where the balcony once had stood and peered down. He then inspected the crumbled debris, looking in several areas, bending down, and moving scraps with his pen. What he didn't find was an open question … but it was soon to be answered.

Chapter 3

Another Kill

BILLY HAD TO CONFRONT the accusations of an eighty-four-year-old parishioner, Connie O'Reilly, a witness to his affair with Mary Peters, and perhaps with Mrs. Owens, the church secretary. Was she sufficiently troubled to relate her concerns to the bishop? She could give him an earful about the monsignor's suspicions of the priest's behavior.

First, he had to confirm that the detective assigned to the balcony collapse concluded it was a regrettable accident. It had the appearance of a chance event, but the investigating detective was about to ask questions that threatened to keep the death of the three priests an open issue.

"Detective Kelly, if there's anything the church can do to close your investigation, please don't hesitate to petition my assistance."

"Thank you, Father Pratt. One point has me baffled. The balcony was secured into cement with bolts. When I inspected the scene, I found only two; six are missing. I'll be damned, but I can't find any of them."

"That's an easy one to solve, Detective Kelly. I have them. When the area was cleared, I took the liberty of trying to find the cause of the collapse. I picked up the bolts and put them in a cup. Let me fetch them for you," said the killer, scampering to his room. He soon returned and handed the cup to the detective.

"Thank you, Father Pratt. Now I can carry through with my report."

"The church will need a copy of the write-up for insurance purposes."

"No problem, Father, and thank you for your help. You have my condolences for your loss."

The detective returned to his precinct, where he emptied the plastic cup of bolts on his desk. He examined them, comparing them to the two he'd recovered from the debris. The bolts from the scene were bent and the channels filled with old cement, but the six Father Pratt had given him were straight, with far less channel debris. Kelly decided to corroborate his findings with the Forensics Department. The conclusion: the six bolts were not collateral damage from the collapsing balcony but had been removed prior to the priests' fall from the second floor. He discussed his findings with his partner, Maggie Burns, asking for her input before bringing it to the attention of their captain. It was one thing for the deaths of the three priests to be declared a tragic accident but … premeditated murder?

"Mike, who would intentionally kill three priests? What would be the possible motive?" his partner asked.

"I haven't got a clue for a motive, but I do have a possible suspect."

"Oh?"

"The priest who gave me the missing bolts, Father Pratt."

"What? Why would he kill three of his brethren?"

"That's what I intend to find out. But what if his intention wasn't three priests? Perhaps one or two were collateral damage? Whatever the case, he lied to me, and I need to know why."

"Are we taking this to the captain?" Maggie asked.

"Not yet. Let's get our ducks in order first. You and I are going back to the church and talk to the good father and the rectory caretaker. Let's see if they can shed some light. You speak to Mrs. Owens separately and away from Pratt."

Father Pratt met with the two detectives the next morning. When they asked about the discrepancy with the bolts, he simply said, "I have no explanation for that." Pratt felt confident in his response, as he believed it would be impossible to prove that he had a hand in the collapse of the balcony.

Detective Burns provided insight to a possible motive to her partner on the drive back to the precinct. "Get this, Mike. Mrs. Owens claims that the monsignor had it in for Pratt. He suspected the priest was making evening visits to a female parishioner—so much so that he demanded Father Pratt keep a detailed journal of his coming and goings outside of the church. According to Mrs. Owens, the monsignor actually called the woman—Pratt had been giving her … let's call it 'special counsel,' when her husband was at work."

"Did she say who the woman was or whether the monsignor's suspicions were warranted?"

"No, but Mrs. Owens said the relationship between Gaston and Pratt was badly frayed. The monsignor had threatened to send Pratt to some isolated parish. If the guy was fooling around, it might be a motive to silence Gaston. Your theory of the other two priests being collateral damage makes sense. According to Mrs. Owens, the monsignor gave his special blessing every Tuesday at noon—alone. But for some unknown reason, Father Simon and Father Ralph both took part in the last blessing."

"Maggie, we have to find out who the woman was that the monsignor called," said Mike.

"Anticipated that. Her name is Mrs. Mary Peters. She lives just a few blocks from the church. We should have a talk with Mary."

Billy was feeling the fallout of Gaston's death. The bishop's office called to summon him for a meeting on Monday at ten in the morning. The detectives hadn't yet declared the deaths of the priests an accident. Mary Peters left a message with Mrs. Owens for Billy to call her. Moreover, he had to address Connie O'Reilly's revelation in the confessional.

The first call he made was to Mary. Although Billy was agitated, Mary was in a panic—Detective Kelly wanted to interview her regarding her relationship with Billy.

"Don't be concerned," Billy said. "Give them the same answers you gave the monsignor—that I've been helping to solve a family issue. By the way, do you know Connie O'Reilly?"

"Everyone within earshot knows her," Mary said, "She's that boisterous woman who lives in the building across the street. Why?"

"She's a parishioner who requested my help." The less Mary knew, he realized, the less she could reveal to the detectives. They could conclude only that he was having an affair with a parishioner, hardly a criminal act.

With the monsignor dead, Billy had a clear path to continue his life of debauchery, but another person could derail his path—Mrs. O'Reilly. He called her on Thursday morning, disguising his voice and saying he was from the bishop's office.

"I wonder if I might come to your residence this evening at nine o'clock to address your allegations."

"How does the bishop's office know of my accusations?" she asked. "I had planned to inform his office but hadn't yet done so."

"Another parishioner overheard your allegations from outside the confessional and reported the conversation to the bishop's office."

Mrs. O'Reilly was convinced the call was from the diocese, but she still was suspicious. "Why must you come to my home so late in the evening?"

"Prior meetings at the bishop's office won't allow for an earlier appointment."

Mrs. O'Reilly reluctantly agreed to meet with him.

In reality, Billy had carefully orchestrated the day and time, as the forecast predicted heavy showers, and the cover of darkness would make identification practically impossible.

He left the church that chilly March evening at 8:30. He wasn't wearing his clerical dress or collar; instead, he wore jeans, a black hoodie, and a dark raincoat. His fake mustache and red wig—leftovers from the parishioners' children's celebration of Halloween—all but guaranteed anonymity.

Billy took the familiar journey to Mrs. O'Reilly's apartment, directly across from Mary's residence, and once inside the unattended foyer, he looked at the names on the mail slots. There it was—Connie O'Reilly, apartment 232. He walked up the stairs, bowing his head when he passed another resident coming down.

The priest knocked on the door, and when Mrs. O'Reilly opened it, he plunged the eight-inch blade directly into her heart and then upward, killing her instantly.

He was exhilarated as he witnessed the life of his victim vanish. He grinned as Connie O'Reilly gasped her last breath; the terror in her eyes was haunting. He entered the apartment and closed the door. He walked toward the front window and peered out, looking across to Mary's apartment. He went through all the rooms, fabricating the appearance of a robbery gone wrong.

Billy left the building under the cover of darkness and heavy rainfall. He noticed two people exiting Mary Peters's building and was aghast—it was Detective Kelly and another woman. He scurried back to the church and immediately burned the wig and mustache in the basement furnace. He removed his rain-soaked clothing and poured himself a whisky. When the phone rang, Billy instinctively flinched. He answered with trepidation. It was Mrs. Owens, checking to see if she was needed any longer that night.

"I'm fine," he assured her. "I'll see you in the morning." He sipped his drink, concerned but curious about what transpired between Mary and the detectives. He dared not call to ask; it would have begged the question of how he knew detectives had been there.

The elimination of Mrs. O'Reilly was Pratt's second premeditated killing. There was no remorse in this despicable man. He killed merely to continue his indulgence without interruption or threat of exposure. He could have resigned from the priesthood, but it was the perfect marketplace for his pleasures; the confessional was his feeding ground.

Billy had to face the bishop on Monday, and he wondered about the agenda. *Will it be a discussion of Gaston's replacement, or will it be related to the previously held meeting between the monsignor and the bishop?*

During Friday morning mass, Pratt's homily addressed the monsignor's death. There were more parishioners in attendance than normal, all curious how the young priest would explain the event and the future of the parish. To Billy's dismay, he noticed Detective Kelly and the same woman he had seen leaving Mary's apartment building seated in the front pew. It was somewhat unsettling, although he perceived it as a police tactic to somehow intimidate him. When the detectives joined the receiving line for communion and approached the priest, they both held their hands out while staring directly into the killer's eyes.

After the services, Kelly asked to meet with Pratt.

"Could you return in three hours or so?" Billy asked. "Important church matters require my immediate attention. The bishop hasn't assigned other priests to the parish yet, so I'm somewhat overwhelmed."

They agreed to meet at noon in the church rectory.

Billy called Mary but didn't mention that he knew she'd met with the detectives on the previous evening.

"Can you see me this evening?" she asked. "My husband is working through the morning."

Billy's response to her request was a bitter disappointment. "I think we should suspend our meetings for a while. With Gaston's death, the detectives are snooping around the church."

"Detective Kelly and his partner were at my apartment last night," Mary said, "asking about my relationship with you."

"What did you tell them?" Billy asked.

"I gave them the same answer I gave the monsignor," Mary said.

She then told him about the robbery and killing of Mrs. O'Reilly; Billy feigned shock at the news.

"The police have an eyewitness," Mary said, "a man who passed the killer in the hallway. It's the gossip of the community."

"I didn't know her very well but knew of her through conversations with Father Simon and Father Ralph," Billy said. "I'm sure the detectives will ask me for information regarding her passing, the poor soul."

"Why are they seeing you, Billy?" Mary sounded surprised.

"Doing what detectives do—find as much information about the victim as they can, hoping for a lead to her killer," he responded. "I'll call again when things are settled in at the church."

"When?" Mary asked, pushing for a commitment.

"It probably will be next week."

Mary was disheartened by the interruption to her social escape and was unprepared for the complications of an affair.

"Father Pratt, this is my partner, Maggie Burns. I'm still somewhat confused about the event that took the lives of Monsignor Gaston, Father Ralph, and Father Simon," said Detective Kelly.

Maggie Burns carefully observed the priest's body language.

Billy noticed that the detective didn't use the word *accident* when referring to the deaths of the three priests but *event*. "How so?" he asked.

"It's the six bolts you gave me, Father."

"What about them?" Billy asked, sitting back in his chair.

"You see, Father, my forensic guys are telling me that it wasn't possible for those fasteners to come down with the balcony. They believe they were taken out beforehand," said the lead detective.

Billy showed no reaction. He knew from the direction of the conversation that he was in their crosshairs. What he was about to say would determine if he would continue to be their prime suspect.

Chapter 4
The Other Man

"**P**ERHAPS YOU SHOULD SPEAK to our maintenance man, Hector. He gave me the cup of bolts."

Billy's startling statement had both detectives dumbfounded, and each eyeballed the other.

"Father, wait—you previously stated that you picked up the bolts at the scene and put them in a cup. Now you're saying the maintenance man gave them to you? Why didn't you tell me that in our previous conversation?" Kelly demanded. The priest had raised the specter of guilt.

"My simple answer, Detective—I just didn't think of it."

"We'd like to speak to Hector right now!" Maggie Burns barked, clearly angry and suspicious of the priest. Her partner placed his hand on her forearm, a message of restraint.

"Detective Burns, your tone is somewhat belligerent and not appreciated," Billy said.

"Forgive my partner's impetuous reaction, Father," Kelly said. "It's just frustrating when new information suddenly appears and sometimes meets the criteria of convenience. Not to say this is the case, but I'm sure you can appreciate our anxiety. Now, when would it be convenient for us to talk to Hector?"

The priest gave a wry smile and sat up in his chair, ready for the next move in this cat-and-mouse game. "Today is Hector's day off, but if it's imperative that you speak to him today, Mrs. Owens will give you his address."

"Thank you, Father. By the way, are you aware that one of your parishioners was murdered last night?" Kelly asked.

"No, I wasn't. Who was she?"

"Father, you said *she*. How did you know I was speaking of a female parishioner?" Detective Burns asked.

Had Billy made a fatal mistake? Or could he slip out of the apparent misstep? "I'm a fan of mystery and do a lot of reading on the subject. It gives me a better perspective on why people take another's life. Statistics prove that men who kill outnumber women who kill by a four-to-one ratio. I just assumed that the poor parishioner was a female victim."

Detective Kelly glanced at his partner as he stood. He thanked the priest for his cooperation and then asked to see Mrs. Owens.

She was nowhere to be found, but a note on her desk indicated she was doing her shopping chores and would be back to the rectory by two o'clock. The detectives decided they would return to speak to the caretaker.

Billy left the church from the rear entrance. Hector's residence was a short walk from the rectory. It was 12:45 P. M.

"Father Pratt, I'm surprised to see you," said Hector, a mentally challenged sixty eight year old. "Please come in and sit."

Billy explained that the police were going to ask Hector about the cup of bolts he'd given the priest.

Hector scratched his head. "I don't remember doing that, but if you say I did, then I accept it as being done."

Billy also told Hector not to tell the police that he'd come to his apartment. "I'm playing a game with them," Billy said, "so I don't want them to know."

Hector smiled. "It'll be our secret," he assured his priest.

Billy shook Hector's hand and left, returning to the church. He entered through the back door and went directly to his office.

Mrs. Owens, her hands grasping two bags, returned about the same time the detectives did. They explained what they needed, and she accommodated them after placing the groceries on her desk.

After they left, she walked into Father Pratt's office, explaining that she had given Hector's address to Detective Kelly and his partner. "Is he in some sort of trouble, Father?"

"No, they want to ask him about the accident and the cup of bolts Hector gave me," said the priest.

Kelly and his partner left the church and went directly to the maintenance man's apartment. They questioned him for about an hour before they realized that the mentally challenged man would be no help.

"Do you think Pratt got to Hector?" Detective Burns asked. "He had ample time to walk to the man's apartment and talk with him."

"Maggie, either we have a cold-blooded killer hiding under the cloth, or we're barking up the wrong tree. He gave us the maintenance man without hesitation. But that still doesn't tell us who took those bolts out of the balcony. Maybe our forensic people have it wrong, and somehow—miraculously—they simply popped out clean."

"I don't buy it, Mike. This coy priest is as guilty as sin. I feel it in my gut."

The detective threw up his hands in frustration. "Well, that's not going to be good enough for Captain Brolin, Maggie. We don't have squat in making a case against Pratt. Who knows? Maybe it was some parishioner who had it in for the monsignor."

"Maybe there's a connection with O'Reilly," Maggie suggested. "Maybe she saw something she wasn't supposed to see and threatened the priest in the confessional. I don't buy the robbery gone wrong theory. Her daughter said she didn't have anything of value to steal."

"Maggie, you know junkies get desperate and will do anything for their next fix. They get ten cents on the dollar through a fence. A junkie with a hundred dollar a day habit has to steal a thousand dollars a day, 365 days a year. Maybe Mrs. O'Reilly was a victim of a junkie's desperation."

The detective's theory seemed plausible, but his partner didn't buy the premise. There was something about Billy that rubbed Maggie the wrong way. He seemed cocky and arrogant, and he had a choreographed answer for every question. Her sixth sense pointed to the priest as a killer, and she was determined to prove it.

"Father Pratt, before Monsignor Gaston's passing, he had certain reservations about your commitment to the priesthood," said Bishop Murphy. "In fact, he thought transferring you to a parish where outside influences were minimal might be beneficial. Do you agree with his proposal—that meditation might resolve the issue?"

"Bishop, I have no reservations about who I am and my service to the Lord," Billy answered. "The monsignor—may he rest in peace—and I had our differences in how to best serve the people of our parish. I believe it's important to show the humanity of priests, and I'm convinced this can be accomplished by interacting with our parishioners. Monsignor objected to the concept, and I feel it was simply our different philosophies, rather than my commitment to the service of the Lord."

"That may be so, Father Pratt, but the head of a parish determines its policies under the direction of your bishop, who answers to the Holy Father. You must understand this chain of command if you wish to survive the vocation you've chosen. I've assigned a new prelate as pastor of Saint Killian's. He's arriving on Thursday. He's a progressive thinker, and you should find him in favor of his priests interacting with parishioners. But be aware, Father Pratt, that we, as priests, live under the close scrutiny of our parishioners, and any hint of impropriety will result in scandal we can ill afford. Do I make myself clear, Father?"

"Perfectly, Bishop Murphy, and I give you my word that I will serve our new pastor and live up to his expectations."

Billy's answer was exactly what the bishop wanted to hear. Saint Killian's was short-handed, and Billy knew his experience in the parish would best serve the incoming monsignor. He left for the church, and when he arrived, he immediately called Mary.

When her husband answered the phone, Billy thought of hanging up, but with caller ID, he dared not risk the suspicion of his lover's spouse.

"Mr. Peters, this is Father Pratt from Saint Killian's. I'm calling individual parishioners who have showed interest in volunteering for our annual food drive. Could you have Mrs. Peters call Mrs. Owens, our caretaker, if she wishes to pursue in helping the program?"

The unsuspecting husband said he would pass the message to his wife. Two hours later, Mary called Billy. Both were desperate to see one another, and a liaison was agreed upon. He wanted to see Mary before the new pastor arrived on Thursday, when he expected his whereabouts would be closely scrutinized.

When he arrived at Mary's apartment on Wednesday evening, he was shocked when the door opened, and standing on the other side was Harry Peters. The priest didn't know what to expect. Had the husband uncovered his involvement with Mary? Why didn't she call to warn him that her husband would be home? He was shaken and fearful that his world was about to crumble.

Then, Harry reached for his coat, saying, "Forgive me, Father for leaving so abruptly, but I'm running late for work."

Billy exhaled a sigh of relief and thanked Harry for allowing his wife to participate in the food drive. They shook hands, and after the door closed, Mary went to the window, confirming that her husband was leaving the building and taking his regular path to work.

"Billy, I'm so sorry. I couldn't call to delay the timing of your arrival. He's generally a predictable person, but for some unknown reason—oh, I can't."

"What is it, Mary?"

She turned away, holding her face in the palms of her hands.

"Mary, please," the priest implored.

"He … wanted to make love, and my reluctance didn't deter him. I'm so sorry, Billy."

"Mary, you have nothing to regret. We discussed this earlier. If we're to be discreet, he cannot be suspicious because of your refusal to accommodate him."

The vision of Mary with her husband excited the wayward priest. He reached for her and kissed her. Their hands explored each other until their passions spilled over, and they retreated to the bedroom. They lay side by side, gasping for air, their cravings reaching a desirable conclusion.

Billy turned to Mary, caressing her back with whispering strokes of his long fingers. "I don't know when we can next meet," he told her. "I first need to get a feel for the new monsignor. He arrives tomorrow, and I expect he'll closely watch my comings and goings."

Mary understood but wasn't happy at the prospect of a prolonged separation. Billy reiterated the importance of her accommodating Harry and avoiding suspicion of infidelity. "Mrs. Owens will be calling you to confirm your participation in the parish food drive," he said.

They kissed passionately, and then he left for Saint Killian's. When he arrived at the church, it was nine thirty. There was a message from Christian DeVoe on his desk, which the priest ignored.

The new prelate arrived on Thursday morning, as scheduled. After a brief meeting with Mrs. Owens, he asked that Father Pratt come to his office. Billy approached the new authority of Saint Killian's, not knowing what to expect. Would the new monsignor make his life so restrictive that there would be no alternative but to leave the priesthood?

When he entered the office, Billy's face lit up; he had hit the jackpot. It was

Father Douglas, his former parish priest, the man most influential in convincing Billy to join the order.

"Father—excuse me, Monsignor Douglas—it's so good to see you. When was the honor bestowed upon you?"

"Billy, it was almost two years after you entered the seminary. It came as a complete surprise, an appointment I couldn't refuse. So tell me, Father Pratt, why did Gaston dislike you so much? I know he was old school, but he was highly regarded within the order."

"Do you remember our first conversation, when I asked you about celibacy and that it would be my deterrent in joining the priesthood?"

"Yes, Billy, and I presume you've been dipping into the cookie jar."

They spoke for nearly an hour. The new monsignor became aware of Billy's difficulties with his predecessor and understood why. The prelate put Billy at ease, agreeing on the importance of priests reaching out to the community. Still, he emphasized the penalization exacted against the church if a misstep were to occur. It seemed that the new monsignor was giving his steward a pass-go sign but warning him to stay out-of-jail.

Over the following six months, Monsignor Douglas added three more priests to Saint Killian's. During that time, Billy's gluttony was unabated. His time with Mary continued, as it did with other parishioners of the confessional. But a former member of the parish, Christian DeVoe, was found hanging from the rafters of his parents' garage. There was no note, but his friends indicated that he was despondent over being abandoned by his lover. The case was ruled a suicide.

The investigating detectives in the death of the three priests were pressured to close the case as an apparent accident; Mrs. O'Reilly's murder was still an unsolved homicide. Detective Maggie Burns was convinced that Saint Killian's had a murderer priest within its walls, and she had a plan to prove her theory.

Chapter 5

Another Victim

"BLESS ME FATHER, FOR I have sinned, and it's been six years since my last confession." A prolonged silence followed.

"Yes my child, continue," said Father Pratt.

"I recently divorced my husband, and I'm having difficulty coping with the loneliness of separation. We have no children, and that was part of our problem. When we married, he was in favor of starting a family after two years, but when the time had passed, and I renewed the topic, he simply dismissed the issue. He said he never wanted to have kids, that they'd ruin our lives. It's been six months since our divorce, and I find the solitude frightening. Father, I'm at my wit's end and afraid of my loneliness. I'm in the gym every day after work to relieve the tension, but I have difficulty sleeping at night."

"I understand, my child. What is your name?"

"Julie."

"I empathize with your desperation and would like to help you. We have a program in which our parish priests visit the homes of parishioners who have a special need and provide counseling that is suitable to each individual situation. Does that sound like something that might interest you?"

"Surely, Father. How do I apply?"

"Julie, we'll need a number where you can be reached so Mrs. Owens—she's our caretaker—or one of our priests might call you?" Pratt wrote her number down on a small pad retrieved from his pocket. "Do you have a good relationship with the other employees at work, Julie?"

"Yes, I do, but I have a very difficult job. I love my faith and my church, but I deplore those who hide behind the cloth to commit unspeakable crimes—people who prey on those in trouble, priests who are predators."

"Who are you?" demanded the startled cleric.

"I'm the detective who's going to nail your ass for killing at least four people and possibly five. Now I know how you get to your victims, you sick bastard—luring them for your own use when they seek comfort from their priest."

"Detective Burns, how dare you enter the sanctity of the confessional under false pretenses."

"How dare you hide behind the cloth for your own sick and perverse life. The collar around your neck is tattered and stained with shame. Know this, priest: I'll be watching you twenty-four/seven, and when you trip, I'll be there with the bracelets!" Maggie shouted, storming out of the confessional. Awaiting parishioners had gotten an earful, and their priest left in a huff.

Billy went to his room and slammed his garments to the floor. He couldn't have Burns shadowing his every move. He surmised that her actions were not sanctioned by her department and that she was a rogue detective who wouldn't let go of her suspicions. He paced the floor for what seemed like an eternity, incensed, planning her demise in various scenarios, none of which was plausible.

Perhaps a call to her superior, complaining of her harassment, is a better alternative—a less dangerous undertaking, he thought. "Yes, that makes more sense," he muttered. "A stern warning of police harassment should do the trick, and the other alternative is always open." He questioned if he should make the complaint or ask the monsignor to intercede. But getting the prelate involved could result in opening himself to never-ending questions. He decided to make the call himself and did so immediately.

Billy's call was directed to Captain Brolin, Maggie Burns's immediate supervisor. Billy described her invasion of the confessional under false pretenses. "As a priest, I forgive her actions but I don't condone her behavior. I would like her restrained from the church and from me, unless it's in an official capacity."

The call resulted in the captain's prompt action. "Burns, have you lost it completely?" he stormed at her. "And you, Kelly, please tell me that you didn't buy what she did."

"Captain Brolin, this guy is a killer hiding behind the protection of the church. I feel it right here!" Maggie said, her fist to her chest.

"Burns, let me remind you of basic detective work—motive and evidence you can present to the district attorney for prosecution. That's how you nail and convict a criminal. What did you expect from the priest? A confession in the confessional?"

"Captain, I wanted him to know that we were going to be up his ass twenty-four/seven, and maybe that will prevent him from killing another innocent. In the meantime, we can find the evidence."

"Did I stutter? It's a nice theory, but it's not 101 by the book. Motive and evidence, Detective. Give me your gun and shield. You're suspended for a month without pay, and this is from the commander's office. You're lucky not to be demoted. His specific words were, 'You tell that loose cannon of yours that if she pulls another stunt like that, she can apply for a crossing-guard position.' Is that clear enough for you, Maggie? And Mike, where were you in her thinking? You're supposed to be partners and confer on investigations."

"Captain, I trust Maggie's instincts, and I agree that this guy is dirty and will kill again."

"Then do it by the book and consider the organization you're up against. Now, both of you get the hell out of here."

Both detectives exited his office.

"Maggie, coffee in five minutes at the diner," Kelly demanded.

"Mike …" she started, but her partner stomped away, waving his arm in disgust.

The diner was minutes from the precinct. Kelly arrived first and took a booth in the rear; Maggie arrived shortly thereafter. She knew what to expect, and the conversation wasn't going to be about the weather. They were more than partners and had been for two years. Mike was forty-nine years old and a twenty-five year veteran of the force. He was a handsome man of Irish descent, standing six feet and weighing one-hundred-eight-two pounds. His eyes were blue, his hair rustic, and he had a fair complexion. Twice divorced, his unusual hours had forced his former wives to seek attention elsewhere; both left him for men with nine-to-five jobs. The only consolation was that there were no children to support. His passions were clothes and his bookie. Mike was an impeccable dresser, and when he wasn't paying for gambling debts, he was spending his money on the latest men's fashion.

"Kelly, I hope you're a better cop than the losers you bet on," said his bookie.

"Pete, just take the plays and scrap the sarcasm," Mike said, tightening his grip on the phone.

"Hey, you paid for my last vacation, but your tab is getting a bit frosty, and the juice isn't cheap."

"Have I ever stiffed my payments?" Kelly snapped.

"No, and I like you my friend, but you know the deal. Cop or no cop, I don't wanna be in the position of sending my collectors for payment."

"Did I just hear a threat from you?"

"Mike, I don't make threats. I just collect what's mine. You're in to me for fifteen large. I'll take your action today, but you're cut off until I'm paid. No hard feelings; it's just business."

"Maybe I have to find a new bookie, Pete."

"Be my guest, Mike, but the other books in town aren't as understanding as me." The gangster disconnected the FaceTime conversation.

Maggie's story was a bit more tragic. She joined the force at twenty-five and was married two years later, giving birth to a baby girl a year afterward. While on routine patrol, she heard the screeching before the deafening collision; the sound resonated for blocks. She ran toward the corner along Dorchester Avenue and turned onto Park Street. When she saw the two vehicles involved in the collision, she was horrified. "No, no, please, God, no!" she screamed. Her husband and daughter were both killed when an eighty-five-year-old woman lost control of her car and slammed into her husband's vehicle. Maggie was given bereavement leave, and when she returned, earned her detective shield when she stopped an armed robbery in the Beacon Hill section of town; she shot and killed the felon before he could harm a hostage.

Maggie was an attractive woman, also of Irish descent. She was a slim five-five; her eyes were green, her hair was blonde and cut just below her jawline. When she was teamed up with Mike, it was strictly business for the first year of their partnership. But the relationship grew as their dependence upon one another kept them alive on more than one occasion. It was against department rules for involved romantic partners or spouses to work together, so they kept their relationship to themselves, but they soon found they had a commonality—both were hard-headed and unwavering.

"Mike, before you say anything, let me explain," pleaded Maggie.

"There's no reasonable explanation for what you did or—more important—for leaving me out of the equation. You not only put your ass on the line but mine as well."

Maggie slumped her head, gathering her response and not wanting to further incite the situation. The detective knew she was wrong, but her outrage for the crimes committed by the priest, as well as his pompous attitude, stripped her of prudent judgment. Maggie didn't dodge the issue; she gained control of her approach and admitted her actions were over the top. In trying to lighten the tension, she said, "You must admit it was a creative approach, and I did have the opportunity to confess a sin."

"Oh yeah? What was that? Stupidity?"

"Well, smart-ass, the priest hit on me. He asked for my number and said Mrs. Owens or another priest would call. Mrs. Owens—she's the caretaker and knows more than she'd admit. Look, Mike, I have the month off and—"

"No, Maggie, whatever you're thinking, forget about it. One more misstep and it's over for you. Remember, this is a Catholic city, and going after one of their own ... well, it's downright suicidal."

"This is one bad dude we're dealing with. You and I know that if he's not stopped, he'll kill again. There's got to be a way before that happens."

"Think about what we have—squat. No motive, no murder weapon. Some misplaced bolts isn't going to do it."

"I spooked him, and when a killer's exposed, he makes mistakes."

"Yeah, or they go ghost, and that could mean he does nothing for months or even years. Serial killers can be active and then disappear before they return to kill again," Kelly reminded her.

"I have an idea. What if ... we use a civilian to do what I did? Set him up with someone whose story is irresistible."

"A civilian? Have you lost it completely?"

"Hear me out. We already have a good relationship with a perfect shill, someone who can take care of herself and owes us. How many times could we have busted Savannah and her girls?"

"Are you kidding? You want a working girl to sit in a confessional and lure a priest? Whatever you're smoking, give it up because you're not talking sense. Even if she got him to make a move on her, she's not a credible witness. The church's lawyers would have a field day."

"We don't know how this dirtbag's superiors feel about him. What if Gaston had something on the priest and was a threat? There's your motive. Maybe Connie O'Reilly saw something and threatened to expose the priest. Remember, her apartment is directly across from the Peters' building."

Maggie kept trying to justify her actions, but Mike reminded her that all she had were suppositions without facts. He agreed that Pratt was a killer but not with Maggie's approach in gathering evidence. He had more experience in this type of case and had seen a few thrown out of court for aggressive and emotional tactics, leading to the acquittal of the accused felon. He asked his partner to go home and take the suspension time to recharge her batteries.

Maggie had no intention of surrendering her instincts. She would be reminded of the priest every night when Mike returned home from a day on the job. They shared a modest rented house on the north side of Boston and were content to live together with no commitments about the future. Mike was a two-time loser on the marriage circuit and didn't want to strike out a third time. He was more of a nester than Maggie. He was a former star athlete in high school and college. A good day was coming home in one piece and watching a Red Sox baseball game while sipping a cold beer.

It was about eight o'clock when Mike arrived home. Maggie was in her pajamas on the couch, watching television.

"Are you hungry?" she asked.

"I already had a sandwich at the diner," he said, "with the detective assigned to me as your replacement."

After he showered, they talked for a couple of hours about his day and the new detective, a newly appointed gold shield. Maggie avoided discussing the Pratt case; she didn't want to carry their differences into the bedroom—at least, not that evening.

After satisfying their sexual appetites, the two detectives retired for the evening. Maggie fell into a deep sleep, but Mike tossed and turned most of the night. It was about 1:30 in the morning when he had a dream of Maggie leaving their bed to investigate a noise in the kitchen.

She put on her robe and quietly left the bedroom, closing the door to avoid waking her partner. When she turned on the light in the kitchen, there was Pickles, her cat, on the counter and looking guilty—he had knocked a spoon to the floor after licking the residue of honey on it. Maggie bent down to pick up the spoon, and as she rose, a hand clasped her mouth and a knife was at her throat.

"You couldn't mind your own business. You had to come to my home, my church, my confessional, and now you're going to pay for your stupidity."

The blade cut deep from one ear to the other; her carotid artery was severed, and Maggie's blood spattered across the room. Billy held her body upright until it was lifeless and then slowly laid it down on the kitchen floor-the killer priest wasn't satisfied that his tormentor was suspended. He envisioned an ongoing attack by the detective that would lead to his ultimate exposure. He quickly slipped from the house, gratified he had eliminated his imminent threat. Before returning to Saint Killian's, he disposed of the knife, breaking the handle from the blade and tossed one piece into the river and the other in a sewer. He burned his clothes and sneakers in the church furnace to avoid any DNA exposure. It was three in the morning before he retired; he was awakened by Mrs. Owens's knock on the door to prepare for the six o'clock service.

Mike shadowed the priest's every move in the life-like parody.

"No! No! Maggie!" Mike shrieked at the top of his lungs, holding her lifeless body in his arms. He had warned her of the potential dangers of telling the killer that she intended to pursue him.

Maggie was buried, but her murder was not forgotten. One of their own had been killed, and Captain Brolin agreed to hear Mike out on his belief a priest was responsible for the deaths of other clergy and a civilian.

"Maggie! Maggie!" the terrified detective screamed, his torso catapulting upward.

Maggie, still half asleep, placed a hand on his shoulder. "Mike, what is it?"

"You're alive, Maggie," he said, placing his hands on her face for confirmation.

"What is it, Mike? You're soaked with sweat." She placed her arms around him and felt his trembling.

"What a dream—it was goddamn terrifying, Maggie. It was so real. I saw him get rid of the knife that he used to kill you and then conduct mass the next day like nothing had happened. I held you in my arms while you were bleeding to death, and I was helpless to save you. It seemed so real and vivid, down to the very details."

"That bastard has gotten into both of our heads," Maggie said. "We have to come up with something to get him before your dream becomes a reality."

Chapter 6

The Plot

WHEN MAGGIE'S SUSPENSION WAS lifted, it came with a stern warning from her captain to stay away from the priest. She had convinced her partner to go along with her previous plan of using a protected "working girl" to trap the killer.

They called Savannah and arranged to meet her at two o'clock. "And don't worry; you're not in trouble," Maggie assured her. "We need your help."

The lady of the night didn't hesitate to accommodate them; she liked being owed a favor by the police.

When the squad car pulled along the curb, Savannah got into the back seat, and the detectives drove to an abandoned railroad depot.

Savannah Moraine was a Louisiana transplant who had moved to Boston for more fertile business opportunities—after the Baton Rouge authorities had requested that she take her trade elsewhere. Now thirty-two, she was her own pimp and controlled five other working girls. Savannah was a classy and sophisticated-looking woman. She stood tall at six feet, taller in heels, and was a slim one-hundred-forty pounds. Her hair was sandy, cropped along her neckline and complemented by hazel eyes.

Her clientele was not off-the-street customers but influential pillars of the community who were willing to pay five-hundred-dollars per hour. Breakfast in the morning would cost the client five-thousand-dollars, which, although steep, was accepted by out-of-town businessmen and women attending a convention. Payment was always made in advance. Most customers were referrals from clients, attorneys, or politicians. The hotels where the business was conducted were in the prominent parts of town, and key receptionists were on Savannah's payroll to ensure discretion. She had been on the streets since she was a teenager after her adoptive parents disowned her following several incidents with the police.

No stranger to the dangers of her profession, Savannah was intrigued by the detectives' proposal. But nothing was free in her business; she asked for protection from a competitor who was threatening her girls. In addition, a cop was harassing Savannah on a weekly basis; he'd demanded money from her if she wanted to avoid being arrested.

Mike assured her that her requests would be dealt with by the end of the next day. Both detectives warned Savannah not to underestimate the priest, that he was a killer and wouldn't hesitate to kill again if threatened by exposure. The three plotted out the plan, which would be in place within the week. It was clever and diabolical, but they agreed it was necessary to fight fire with fire, and it had to be off the grid, as it would not be sanctioned by their captain. Both detectives knew they were putting their careers on the line.

Savannah rented an apartment blocks from Saint Killian's, as her hotel was not a convincing residence for a member of the parish. It was Friday; she would visit the confessional the following afternoon—the first step in trapping the killer priest.

Kelly and Burns visited the cop who was demanding protection money from Savannah. They convinced the patrolman that it would be detrimental to his career if he ever approached their informant again, and they threatened to report him to internal affairs, which would result in dismissal and/or jail time for extortion.

Next, they visited the pimp who was trying to muscle in on Savannah's business. When they drove up to his collection area, Kelly and Burns demanded he visit the back of their car, and several locals observed the process. He was given two choices, both of which would inflict severe punishment. One choice was that he could stick to his own territory or face daily harassment, resulting in a severe cash-flow problem. The other was that they would spread the word that he was a confidential informant, and they would visit him weekly, giving the appearance that he was working with the police. That would not only result in negative cash flow but retribution from those who would eliminate police informants with their own court of justice.

Savannah had a clear path to follow, now that she was no longer concerned with the threat of paying protection money to a corrupt cop or a competitor.

On this pleasant May afternoon, Savannah's attire was conservative as she approached Saint Killian's to start the first phase of the plan. She entered the front door and proceeded to the confessional, standing in line behind two other women. She was nervous and internally rehearsing her script. She had played roles with paying customers, often times faking their abilities as men while satisfying their fantasies. An occasional client played rough but was subdued, when needed, by paid bodyguards, and the culprit would be denied future access.

This encounter would be different, and, at times, she questioned the value of her agreement with Kelly and Burns. But here she was, and there was no turning back. If she reneged, it would end her time in Boston and result in her fleeing to another city to reestablish her business.

Ten minutes later, Savannah entered the confessional and said, "Bless me father for I have sinned. It's been twenty years since my last confession."

"That's a considerable time since your last acknowledgment of sins. May I ask why, my child?"

The plot began as planned. She told a story of being an orphan who experienced abuse in the foster homes where she was placed. She blamed God for turning his back on her and for her feeling scarred, inadequate, and sexually unsatisfied in any of her scurrilous relationships. Savannah said she was looking for a new beginning and was a recent member of the parish.

"And why do you suddenly feel the need for confession?" he asked.

"Because the alternative is the unthinkable. I recognize the need for help and forgiveness. It's been a lonely time in my life," she said.

"What's your name, my child?" he asked.

"Savannah."

"Well, Savannah, welcome to our parish. I hope to see you at my nine-thirty mass tomorrow. For your penance, say ten Hail Marys and ten Our Fathers."

"Thank you, Father."

When Savannah left, the priest carefully pulled the curtain in the confessional aside, eyeing his recent confessor. He was pleased by her appearance, but his last encounter with Maggie Burns had put a caution flag to his approach. He no longer accepted first impressions as his gospel. If she continued as a parishioner seeking reconciliation, he would guide her, as he often did with others on a personal level.

After leaving the confessional, Savannah sat in one of the pews directly across from the booth. The priest observed her kneeling and reciting her prayers. He continued to look, as no one was in line to his confessional. Billy, now exited, smiled at parishioners but took special notice of the attractive Savannah. Within five minutes, she had left the church for her newly rented apartment. She called Mike and Maggie from her cell phone, explaining the priest seemed to have taken the bait but with caution.

"How do you know, Savannah?" Mike asked.

"When you've been in this line of business for any time, you know when a guy's juices are flowing. He'll be mine the next time I'm in that confessional. We'll just have to wait until next Saturday, but that will give me time to meet with my girls and explain my absence."

"Don't tell them what you're doing. Make up any story you'd like but the real one," Maggie cautioned.

"Not to worry, guys; it's not my first journey around the block," Savannah said.

The priest had been passive in his activities since the encounter with Maggie Burns. He continued to see Mary Peters, although his visits were decreasing, which became troubling for his anxious mistress, who wanted out of her marriage but was fearful of being abandoned by her lover if she pressed the issue.

It was time for Savannah to pursue the plan choreographed by Kelly and Burns. She entered the confessional and blessed herself.

"Father, I want thank you for your patience and for providing comfort in my despair. I really haven't anything to confess since last week, but I did want to take the opportunity to let you know how I feel."

"I'm sorry, but I don't know who you are, my child." The priest was intentionally coy, but he was almost certain it was Savannah in the confessional.

The lady of the night continued to play the game. "Oh, I'm so sorry, Father Pratt; it's Savannah, Savannah Moraine. We spoke last week."

"Oh yes, Savannah. I'm glad you've made some progress, and I did notice that you attended my nine-thirty mass last Sunday." Savannah, realized the priest broke the sanctity of her anonymity during the confessional. "The bastard peeked," she reasoned.

"Yes, Father, it was up-lifting."

"What do you do, Savannah?"

"I'm in the process of looking for employment and have a positive second interview next week. It's keeping my loneliness from consuming my thoughts."

"Have you engaged yourself socially with others to challenge that sense of loneliness?"

"I'm not very forward, and I'm tired of the bar scene and dating services. I despair the lonely nights. Being alone is the heart of my problem."

"Savannah, the church has a program of home visitations for situations like yours. It involves one-on-one counseling to invigorate your path to self-worth and confidence, while engaging within the community. Would that be of interest to you?"

"It sounds wonderful, Father. How do I move forward?" Savannah asked.

The priest was intrigued with her innocence. It had been a while since his last conquest, and his relationship with Mary Peters was running its course. He wanted to accelerate his meeting with Savannah, but today was impossible because of his committed Saturday schedule. The priest suggested he could visit her the following evening, rather than assigning her to another priest. Savannah, playing the part, showed her gratitude of his compassion and suggested that perhaps he could have dinner at her apartment at six o'clock. The priest accepted, and after giving him her address, she left the confessional, sat in a pew, and recited the penance exacted.

When Savannah reached her apartment, she called Maggie, explaining what had transpired with the priest. She also called a long time customer, who had special talents in video surveillance.

"Be cordial," Maggie told her, "but don't rush the process. He has to swallow the bait."

"I can assure you that I have a plan in mind that will guarantee the priest will come back for more," Savannah said. "I've schooled my own girls that a return client is best for their business." Dealing with repeat customers was safe, and it eliminated the occasional wild card—a guy who liked to hurt people.

When Savannah agreed to cooperate with the detectives, she took on an additional risk beyond her usual threat of possible harm. In order for this plan to work, the priest had to be convinced of his conquest. The only way that could happen was for her to engage in repeated sexual intercourse with a killer.

Savannah had played several roles for customers to satisfy their fantasies, but this one disgusted her. She had to enter the deepest core of the killer, performing acts he hadn't imagined and would not soon forget, her talents imbedded within his sensuality.

On Sunday, Billy was about to leave the rectory for his six o'clock rendezvous with Savannah when Mrs. Owens informed him that Monsignor Douglas wanted to see him. He glanced at his watch and then hurried to the prelate's office. When Billy arrived, the monsignor began to discuss a proposed project to expand Saint Killian's. Billy listened patiently, occasionally glancing at his watch.

It was almost six o'clock, and the conversation with the monsignor showed no sign of ending. Then, he asked Billy for his thoughts on the plan. By the time Billy had offered his opinion to the satisfaction of the prelate, it was 6:20 P.M. He dashed from the church and into his car; the drive took fifteen-minutes.

When he arrived at 6:40 P.M., he apologized to his alluring host and explained his delay.

Savannah didn't flinch. "I completely understand," she said, "and I appreciate your taking time from your busy schedule to help with my state of affairs."

Because Savannah didn't have the culinary skills of most women, she decided to order Chinese food. "I'm not much of a cook," she admitted. "I apologize if my food selection isn't to your taste."

Billy quickly dismissed her concern. "I love Chinese food and haven't indulged in it for some time." In truth, his food preferences were the last thing on his mind.

She placed two bottles of beer on the table, which elicited a smile from the priest.

'How perfect this will be, he thought, *a conquest with no illusions of domestication. She's already made me aware of the shortcomings responsible for her broken relationships. I hope her deficiencies don't extend to the bedroom.*'

They talked for almost two hours, and both agreed to continue her counseling. Savannah was demure throughout the evening, which put the priest at ease.

"Is Wednesday convenient for our next meeting?" Billy asked.

Savannah declined. "I have a doctor's appointment that can't be changed; it took me two weeks to get it."

They then both agreed to another Sunday meeting at six o'clock, pending any last-minute change.

The days passed quickly, and Savannah had every intention of planting her hooks deep into the priest on the seventh day of the week. She had ordered a pizza for dinner, which didn't faze Billy; he was there for the conquest of his parishioner's body.

The conversation started to drift toward a personal nature, and the occasional reassuring touches became more suggestive. When Savannah rose from the table, the priest reached for her hand—the moment had arrived. Within minutes, they retreated to the bedroom, and the priest soon found that her sexual prowess exceeded his expectations. He was delirious, and after a brief respite, he continued his frenzy. Savannah's experience provided the aphrodisiac that would haunt the priest during every hour he was away from his newfound conquest.

She, on the other hand, felt nothing but contempt for the killer, but she played her role to perfection.

"Yes, I have the video disc," Savannah said, when she arranged to meet Burns and Kelly, the camera, cleverly hidden in her bedroom. When the bishop received his copy, Billy and Monsignor Douglas were immediately summoned to his office, though unaware of the purpose of the meeting.

The bishop pointed to the video disc on a small table near his desk. Shaking his head, he revealed the contents, his priest and Savannah engaging in sexual intercourse. Monsignor Douglas covered his face with both hands. Billy was speechless; he'd never suspected that Savannah was a plant.

The bishop had notified Rome before handing down his ruling. Billy was defrocked, and Monsignor Douglas was to be reassigned as pastor of another parish. It was a stunning turn of events for the killer priest, who was ordered to immediately gather his belongings and leave Saint Killian's.

When Billy left the bishop's office, he felt a rage within that threatened his stability. His temples pounded, and he pressed his hands against both sides of his head. He fell to one knee on the steps of the diocese building, trying desperately to relieve his pain. His world was in the midst of collapse, and he wanted to accost the Delilah—and end her life. He was no longer Father Platt, but simply Billy John Pratt, ordinary citizen of Boston.

When Billy reached Saint Killian's, Mrs. Owens gave him a message from Mary Peters; it read, "Urgent." He didn't have the presence of mind to return her call. He immediately started packing his belongings in an army-style duffel bag. It would be another mistake in a day he would never forget. He glanced at his confessional of pleasure as he walked past it on the way toward the entrance of the church. When he opened the door, he was met by Harry Peters, his lover's husband, who immediately placed a gun to Billy's head and identified himself—as if Billy didn't know.

"Don't be foolish," Billy said.

"You're supposed to be a man of God and you're screwing my wife. I knew something was going on—the anonymous calls that said my wife was cheating on me. When I held the gun to her head, she told me it was her priest—you! How could you destroy a family? She was my whole life, and we could have worked it out," said Mr. Peters, clearly distraught. He didn't give the defrocked priest time to utter another word.

The gun exploded, and Billy fell to the ground. Peters placed the gun under his own chin and fired, his body falling on top of his wife's lover.

Harry Peters was pronounced dead on the steps of the church, but Billy somehow survived the point-blank shooting and was transported to the hospital, where emergency surgery was performed. He was placed into an induced coma, and his chances of survival were not encouraging.

Detectives later discovered the body of Mary Peters, shot by her husband before he sought revenge on the priest.

The scandal that ensued from the shootings made for colorful and interesting reading in the press, gossip sheets, and television newscasts. There were no indictments, as Harry Peters had killed his wife, and now both were dead. Billy was seen as a victim of a jealous spouse, as well as yet another priest who cheated on his church and the parishioners.

The innuendos by the news media indicated the defrocked priest was more than just a philanderer. It was noted that the authorities questioned him on the suspicious deaths of three priests and another parishioner. Also brought to light was his participation in homosexual activities with a teenage group of boys, which resulted in the suicide of one of them. The media's source of this information was never revealed, but the high-fives Kelly and Burns gave each other after reading the articles left little doubt.

It wouldn't be the end of the story, as the fallen priest would seek retribution from those who had killed his mistress.

Chapter 7
Retribution

THE EX-PRIEST HAD BEEN hospitalized for thirteen weeks and celebrated his thirty-first birthday with the agony of pain and sin. He engaged in daily rehabilitation, as his brain had to be reoriented on things he'd formerly taken for granted on a daily basis. Learning to walk and speak without slurring his words was punishing, as his brain had been shocked into partial darkness. It was a grueling task, but hatred for his betrayers fueled a determination that bordered on fanaticism. With every exhausting and painful step, his movement was toward an image of those who had betrayed him. He plotted their demise, throwing caution to the wind. He was no longer a priest and had to fend for himself.

One day, the nurse informed Billy that he had visitors. It was the two detectives responsible for his fall from grace, Kelly and Burns.

As they approached his bed, they noticed that the ex-priest's facial hair covered the scars of the fateful shooting, the bullet piercing his cheekbone when the gun in the hand of Harry Peters, slipped below it's intended target.

The fallen priest tried to contain his rage and contempt. "Are you here to gloat detectives or just slumming?"

"Aw, we thought you'd like to see the faces of the people who are going to put you away for life for the murder of four people," Kelly said. "Doesn't that give you a warm and fuzzy feeling inside, knowing that you'll be on our radar twenty-four/ seven when you leave these luxurious accommodations?"

"Go ahead and rejoice in your triumph," Billy snarled, "but remember, there's always a penalty for victory, and the price can be expensive."

"Is that a threat to Boston's finest that I'm hearing?" Kelly asked with a wry smile.

"I don't threaten, Detective. It's never a good policy to forewarn an opponent," Pratt sneered.

"You consider us your adversaries?" Mike asked. "Do you really think we're going to give you an inch of breathing room when you leave this five-star facility? I expect that you and I are going to cultivate a very close relationship. We're going to be so tight that you'll be asking for the name of the cologne I wear, you slime ball."

"Let me ask you a question, killer. Don't you have a scintilla of remorse for killing three of your fellow brethren, or is your soul so dark that it's devoid of compassion and remorse?" Maggie Burns asked.

"You're both boring me, detectives. Just keep this in mind before you take your leave—battles are won before they're fought, and mine … has yet to take hold."

"Do you hear that, Detective Burns? We have a student of Sun Tzu in our midst." Kelly leaned to the side of the priest's head, inches from his ear. "Now you take heed, killer. You're going to pay for what you did, and we'll have the pleasure of watching you gasp your last breath."

"Et tu, Brute, and you be careful, detectives."

The plainclothes officers both sneered as they left the room.

The ex-priest was seething from the exchange. He was certain of what he had to do, and he wasn't going to let Kelly and Burns become his albatross.

One morning, Billy's nurse approached the room to administer his daily medication, only to find an empty bed.

Eleven months passed, and there was no sign of the ex-priest; he'd become a ghost. It was as though he didn't exist—and that had the detectives on edge.

Pratt was still a suspect in multiple homicides, cases that Kelly and Burns continued investigating. After exhausting all airline, bus, and train records, the detectives concluded Pratt had evaded detection. Maggie theorized he'd hitchhiked his way out of the state to avoid toll cameras.

The police couldn't declare an all-points bulletin, as he wasn't a fugitive. Mike Kelly wasn't convinced, as Maggie was, that Pratt had left the state. Kelly felt the priest's homicidal personality would rear up again and that it was just a matter of time before Pratt would reappear—and he was right.

* * *

"Hey, Sanchez, I need four loads of sand for this bunker. Take the truck back to the barn and tell Eduardo to load you up. Make sure he includes the grading rake and shovel," shouted the superintendent of the golf course.

The thirty-two-year-old Sanchez, waved his hand and then entered the truck. It was common practice for landscapers and golf course superintendents to hire undocumented workers. Most were paid below minimum wage and acquired false papers, backed by social security numbers of relatives or dead people.

Billy had found the safe house he needed. The golf course was on the outskirts of Boston, and his appearance had dramatically changed. His brain hadn't fully recovered, so the right side of his face was distorted—one eye and his mouth were flaccid and facial hair masked a good portion of it.

Billy had been working at the golf course for three months and lived in a house for workers on the premises. It was convenient for him and provided the superintendent assurance that most of his men would be on time for work. The house consisted of several bunk beds for the non married workers, although some of the men with families would also employ the convenience if they worked late or weather conditions warranted their staying.

One evening after work, several of the men were sitting at a long table, playing cards. Billy was lying in his lower bunk when a worker called out to him.

"Hey, Sanchez, how come you never join us in cards? Afraid to lose your money?"

Billy didn't respond.

"Hey, motherfucker, I'm talking to you!"

Still, there was no response from the ex-priest.

The young worker rose from the bench seat, shaking off the hands of those who tried to restrain him. He walked to the bunk bed and got into Billy's face, but before he could blink an eye, a switchblade was at his throat, and Billy's hand was behind the coworker's head.

"If you like to see with both eyes," Billy hissed, "I suggest you get back to your card game and consider yourself very fortunate that I'm in a charitable mood today. Understand?"

The worker backed off and returned to the card game. Billy had been tested, and the message was clear. He was a loner, someone the other workers thought was strange, but he avoided confrontation because he didn't want the attention from others. This time was different, though, and he'd given an unchallenged response.

It was August, and before long, Billy would press his plan into motion. Golf season would come to an end in November, and most of the workers would be furloughed until the following March. The superintendent kept a skeleton crew, based on seniority, and Billy surmised that he would be out of work within three months. He had little time to seek his retribution.

Friday nights in Boston were saturated with tourists and locals; it would be an opportune time to blend into a crowd. The weather was perfect for his intentions; a dense fog had surrounded the city. When he approached the front desk of the hotel, he placed a hundred-dollar bill in the receptionist's hand and said, "The lady Moraine, told me to see you."

Billy was given a phone number, which he called from a throw-away phone. He made an appointment with one of Savannah's girls within the hour. It was eight o'clock when he took the elevator to the third floor. He knocked on the door to room 333 and was immediately greeted by a woman in her thirties, dressed in sexy lingerie. She smiled and then got down to business, requesting the five-hundred dollar payment. Billy obliged and was escorted to the bar in the living room. He sat on a stool, sipping the drink that she poured for him. After a brief time, they went to the bedroom and completed the transaction.

"I hope you were satisfied," the lady of pleasure said. "Please request my services the next time you call Savannah."

Those were the last words she would speak before the knife penetrated her heart. The killer vanished in the mist of the night but left an unclouded message.

When the detectives viewed the body of the slain prostitute, they suspected the killer priest had returned. The woman's tongue had been cut from her mouth and replaced with a picture of a canary.

Detective Kelly questioned the receptionist, who gave him a description of a man who had claimed to know Savannah, but he didn't fit Billy Pratt's physical profile. Kelly was at a loss, thinking they might have jumped to conclusions. "Perhaps we're dealing with someone from the victim's past," he suggested.

The detectives then spoke to Savannah.

"Did you receive any phone calls that seemed strange?" Detective Kelly asked. "Can you recall this customer—the one who killed one of your girls?"

"His description doesn't fit any of the regular clients, but it's not unusual to get an out-of-towner looking for a night of joy. Diana was a sweetheart. She wasn't confrontational, but she knew how to handle the aggressive ones. She's been with me for three years," said the tearful Savannah.

"Did she have a boyfriend or a past client with a grudge?" Maggie asked.

"No, she lived with one of the other girls—Susan."

"Can we talk to her? Maybe she can shed some light," Burns said.

Savannah called Susan to ask her to meet with the detectives. When Savannah told her why, Susan screamed, and Savannah heard the girl's cell phone clatter to the floor.

Later, when Maggie questioned Susan, she could shed no light on why someone would harm her friend.

The detectives questioned the receptionist again, asking if he'd noticed any distinguishing marks or tattoos on the man who had gone to Diana's room.

"Yes, now that you mention it," the receptionist said slowly. "He was disfigured. His right eye was saggy, as was his mouth. At least, I think his mouth was saggy—I can't be sure because of his beard."

Kelly and Burns looked at each other and then left the hotel for the hospital where Pratt was treated. They asked the hospital administrator if there were photos taken of the priest before he was discharged, but the hospital supervisor explained that Pratt was never formally discharged; he'd suddenly disappeared in the night. She did however, provide the detectives with the hospital snapshots of Billy. There it was—the ex-priest in full beard, with disfigurement of the eye and mouth, as it was when they'd confronted him in his hospital bed and thrown their warning of close surveillance in his face. They'd never requested the up-to-date photos of the killer when they were investigating his whereabouts; they assumed his physical appearance had changed since the shooting. They both realized that they had dropped the ball in not keeping closer tabs on the ex-priest, but their case load stretched the detectives time in several directions.

Billy returned to the country club. He was gloating, and his intent was clear. Savannah had destroyed his life, and he was going to inflict pain on the betrayer and those around her. He concluded that Kelly and Burns would soon realize that he was the killer. He packed his duffel bag with the few belongings he had, but before leaving, he looked into the mirror. Billy realized that a new description would be given by the police. He put his hand to his beard and decided to shave it off, as well as the hair on his head. He then took two Band-Aids and placed one under his eye and the other to the side of his mouth in an attempt to disguise his disfigurement.

As he was about to leave the house, the young aggressor who had gotten into his face, appeared. It was unfortunate timing for the immature immigrant, who could now identify Billy's new appearance. Billy threw the young man's body down the basement steps, and the killer priest fled.

Kelly and Burns had warned Savannah that she was in grave danger and suggested she disappear from the state. "We can't protect you," Maggie told her. "Our captain refuses to provide the manpower needed to guard a woman who's breaking the law. Detective Kelly and I feel responsible for your state of affairs and regret asking you to risk your life in order to trap the priest. Please go."

"No, thank you, detectives," Savannah said. "Running away isn't an option."

Billy left for the one place he knew he wouldn't be found. He rented space in a self-storage facility under the name of John Foley. It was a ten-by-ten unit and provided heat and air conditioning. He had all the comforts of a rented apartment at a cost of ninety-five dollars per month. He stored a bed, portable chemical toilet, survivor food, and clothes. It was a perfect place to disappear until he determined it was safe to leave the state. He was no longer thinking as a priest but as a criminal on the run from the police. He was now a wanted man, and the police could prove he was a killer.

The ex-priest was obsessed with the idea of retribution and not just for the woman who had bedded him while a hidden camera sealed his faith with the church. His intense hatred extended to Maggie Burns, and that prevented him from leaving the state until payback was imposed.

Billy retired for the evening but was unable to sleep. His past wounds resurfaced, and he wondered if he hadn't been sodomized as a twelve-year-old if fate would have been kinder to him. He placed his hands to his face and mumbled, "Lord, why have you forsaken me?" Billy cried; his soul was shedding, and the inner depths of his being was stripped of all hope. He was no longer a creature of his faith but a fallen angel, doomed to eternal damnation.

The next morning, he listened to the news on his portable radio. The killing was the major story of the broadcast. His name was announced as the killer, an ex-priest. It was time to leave the state … but he would return.

Three Years Later

Billy fled the country and worked as an oil rig hand in Coro, Venezuela, under the alias of Peter Dunn. His hair was shoulder-length, and he sported a goatee. The plastic surgery on the right side of his face was all but healed; it had been performed by the criminal element of an underworld that provided any service for a price, and the thirty-five-year-old's makeover was remarkable. The surgery completely transformed his appearance. He could no longer be recognized as Billy John Pratt. It was time for his return to Boston to complete his deep-seated hatred of those responsible for his banishment from the church and his country. He'd had three long years to plan, and every day of pain that he endured from surgery was a reminder of his task.

Leaving Venezuela was a bit more complicated for him than he'd anticipated. Billy had forged a relationship with a thirty-year-old woman. She was a widow who owned a house—that provided the shelter and anonymity he needed. Maria Lopez was five-foot-three, with black hair and brown eyes. She was a mestizo, the offspring of a Spaniard and South American Indian.

Maria had no children and worked in a local textile factory. She cared for the man called Peter Dunn, who showed a gentle side that had been lost since he was twelve. She asked no questions about his past and provided the sexual endurance he desired.

"Why must you leave? I fear if you do, I'll never see you again, *mi amor.*"

"Maria, I must return to the Unites States to finish business left undone. When it's completed, I promise to come back to you and the life we have," Billy said.

The next day, he informed his foreman, Maria's brother, that he would be leaving Venezuela.

"Peter, *porque*? Does my sister know?"

"Yes, Carlos."

"What's going on, Peter? What's so important in the United States for you to leave?"

"Carlos, it's better that you don't know. It's something that has to be done. I can't explain."

"Can't … or won't, Peter?"

"Take your pick, Carlos," Billy snapped, annoyed at being pressed.

"My sister gave you a life here, and now you're going to discard her like a piece of garbage," Carlos said, grabbing Billy's arm in anger.

"You're taking it the wrong way, Carlos. And I suggest you let go of my arm." Carlos had triggered a central core in the ex-priest, an instinct that was screaming for survival measures.

"Perhaps if I dig a little into who you are and what you ran away from in the United States, you might reconsider leaving," Carlos said, unaware that his fate was hanging in the balance.

"Carlos, have you ever heard the expression, 'Let sleeping dogs lie'?"

"You son of a bitch, have you ever heard of the Columbian necktie? You bed my sister, live in her home, and discard her like trash. I don't think so, my friend." He still had no idea that he had sealed his fate, as well as his sister's.

Billy was now a wanted man in two different countries.

Chapter 8

Payback in Boston

WHEN BILLY RETURNED TO the United States, the brazen killer rented an apartment in the same building where he'd murdered Connie O'Reilly almost four years earlier. With his physical transformation masking his true identity, he could come and go as he pleased.

Billy spent the next two weeks shadowing his intended victim. He kept copious notes, carefully studying the routine of his target; he was fully aware of his distinct advantage. After the killing, the police would immediately draw the conclusion that the former priest of Saint Killian's church had committed the crime—but not Sean O'Sullivan, his new alias.

It was time for retribution. He had waited more than three years for this day, and the city of Boston would scream out for the capture of the killer. Billy knocked on the door of the second-floor apartment and heard an immediate response.

"Just a minute." When the detective opened the door, she smiled and asked, "How can I help you?"

In the next instant, the eight-inch blade found its mark, striking Maggie Burns's heart, killing her instantly.

Billy stepped inside and locked the door—and then he proceeded to leave his message. He cut her tongue from her mouth and attached a picture of a canary. There was no doubt that Mike Kelly would conclude that Billy had committed the crime. This killing, planned for three years, had been executed to perfection.

He peered over her body and then spit on the dead woman's face. He was unconcerned that it would provide DNA evidence against Billy John Pratt. It was part of his plan to announce to Kelly and Savannah Moraine … that they were next on his radar. His emotion was one of exaltation, and he savored the glow of his own pleasure.

Before leaving Maggie's apartment, the ex-priest noticed a picture frame with a photograph of Maggie and Mike on the night table in the bedroom. He smashed the frame and ripped the photo to shreds, leaving the broken shards of glass on the bed and then urinating on the remnants. He left the apartment and walked several blocks before stopping at a coffee shop to order a sandwich and a cup of coffee.

After eating, Billy hailed a cab and gave the driver an address away from his own apartment. He walked the balance of the distance, stopping at the local newsstand to buy the *Boston Herald.* Then he went home, where he sat on his couch, kicked off his shoes, and raised his arms with clenched fists.

The next morning, Billy turned on the television, expecting to hear the account of the murder. There was nothing. "It's too early," he told himself. "Her body probably hasn't been found yet."

But it had—and it was by her lover and partner.

On this Sunday morning, Billy did the unthinkable; he walked to Saint Killian's and attended the eleven o'clock service. When the priest was giving his homily, Billy reflected on when he'd stood at the same podium, performing for his parishioners.

He originally had rejected the idea of becoming a priest, but he later became enamored with the empowerment of the white collar, since tattered by his despicable actions. He'd been comfortable with the role and the perks. The church and the confessional had been his reservoir to feed his sexual appetite. When his world was threatened, he became a killer with no conscious or moral compass.

Two Days Later

"Captain, we have to find the son of a bitch who killed, Maggie." Angry and despondent, Kelly was determined to find the killer. "We know who he is, and for him to come back after three years tells me he's confident that he won't be recognized. I'd bet a year's salary that he's changed his appearance, maybe with the help of surgery."

"Mike, we'll catch the bastard, but it's going to come from solid detective work. If you're right, and he's changed his appearance, we need our sketch artist to work from an old photo of the priest and see how he can help us. Maggie's funeral and the burial is this afternoon. Tomorrow, I want you in my office at nine in the morning to meet with the department artist. You and Maggie were the only ones who were up close to this piece of garbage. Speaking of being up close, I know you guys were more than just partners. I'm truly sorry for your loss, Mike."

"Captain, this is new territory for me. It's never been this personal."

"Maybe you should talk to our chaplain. He's a good guy, and it might be helpful," suggested the captain.

"No, I've had my fill of priests, and there's only one that I want to talk with. I swear by the Almighty that I won't rest until this mutt is caught." Kelly's resolve was imprinted in the heavens; his declaration was loud and clear.

"Mike, I don't know what to say. Technically, I'm supposed to take you off the case, but I won't. Watch your back with this psycho. Until we can identify his appearance, be aware of any new contacts," Captain Brolin warned.

"I'm not the only target of this maniac. Savannah Moraine needs to be informed. Once we have a definitive sketch to work with, I recommend we get the press and public involved."

"We have the full backing by the commissioner, Mike. The priest has crossed the blue line, and he won't get far this time."

Maggie's Eulogy

"Maggie Burns left us too soon. Those who knew her were touched by her infectious smile and her tenacity as a cop. She had dreamed of being on the force since graduating high school. Maggie lived her ambition, first through her father, who served for thirty-years, and then as a first-grade detective. She never came to the job talking about retirement; it was always about solving the next case. We have lost a sister-in-arms; the public has lost a servant who cared. We all bleed blue when one us has fallen, and the way we take solace is to catch the killer. She was my partner … my soul mate, and she will never be forgotten," Mike said, his voice choked with emotion.

Kelly's words at Maggie's funeral were an acknowledgment that they were more than partners in blue, but he also lost more than a mate. She had been his compass, his friend, and his lover. Maggie had understood him, often completing his thought before he spoke. They both accepted the job and the dangers they faced daily, and they always agreed that a good day on the job was coming home unscathed.

Kelly's grief turned to anger, and he wanted payback for Maggie's killing—this would be his mission in life. Memories of her and the scent of her perfume would remind him of each night they'd spent in their apartment as lovers. The ex-priest had to pay the price.

Billy anticipated that his killing the detective would give rise to a strong police response. He was an avid follower of sensational crimes and how the police eventually captured a felon. His study of their techniques gave him the confidence to avoid mistakes that would result in his capture. He concluded it wouldn't be long before a forensic artist would have a sketch posted on all the media outlets. Two more offenders had to pay the price for betrayal, but he realized that would have to wait. Savannah would have been alerted and possibly have police protection. He had the taste of revenge in killing Maggie Burns, and he would need to take great pains to control his desire to deal with Savannah Moraine and Detective Kelly.

Indonesia

The felon would leave Boston and the United States immediately, having preplanned his escape route to a country with no extradition with the United States. It was several days before he arrived in Indonesia with a forged passport. He had enough money to rent an apartment for seventy-five dollars a month and pay for essentials; American dollars were exchanged for several thousand rupiahs, the Indonesian currency.

Billy secured a job as a rigger with an American oil company on the island of Sumatra under the alias of Jeff Casey. Foreign workers weren't welcomed by native Indonesians, as it was tantamount to taking the livelihood away from one of their citizens. His hair was long again, and he sported a full beard. He was a chameleon on the run from two countries, facing certain execution from either one if he was caught.

Police Frustration

The Boston police saturated the media outlets with the forensic sketch of Billy. The only responses were from the landlord who had rented the apartment to the ex-priest and a customs agent, who remembered a person who fit the description. Kelly was astounded that his partner's killer had the tenacity to rent an apartment in the building where he was a suspect in the killing of a former tenant. The breaks were going against the police, as the forensic sketch didn't get posted on the customs checkpoints until after Billy had fled under the name of Sean O'Sullivan. But Kelly was successful in tracking down the country to which Maggie's killer had escaped.

"I'd like to know how an ex-priest can evade the dragnet we had in place. Did he learn that in the seminary?" Captain Brolin was clearly frustrated by the lack of results.

"You know, Captain, I remember a conversation Maggie and I had with him in which he confessed to being an avid fan of criminal history. I can't let this bastard get away from us like this. There's got to be a way of getting to him."

"Mike, he picked a country that has no extradition treaty with the United States. We're screwed," said the captain.

"But we can make his life miserable. We can inform the Indonesian authorities that they have a murderer in their country. The government has taken a hard stance with drug dealers, executing thousands. They might not have an extradition treaty with us, but we can provide enough fodder to solve our problem," Kelly snapped.

"That bastard might cost me, Mike," Brolin replied.

"What do you mean, Cap?"

"The commissioner took a lot of heat from the mayor for failing to nab this guy, and blame has a funny way of rolling downhill. I have a meeting with the commissioner tomorrow morning. I believe you'll be saluting a new captain by the end of the week."

"I hope not, Captain. There wasn't any more that we could have done, and it was by the book."

Kelly reached out to the Indonesian authorities. They appreciated the heads-up but couldn't guarantee punishment for crimes not committed in their country.

Bribery was rampant in Indonesia and Billy was about to discover that life in his safe haven would soon become untenable.

"Hello, is this Chief Tito Arianto?" Kelly asked.

"Yes, it is. Who's calling?"

Kelly offered the details of Billy's criminal history to the chief of the Indonesian police. He listened patiently and then reminded the detective that the two countries did not have an extradition treaty. Kelly acknowledged the fact, but said he was giving the chief a courtesy heads-up from one policeman to another.

"Detective, are you familiar with the meaning of our motto, Rastra Sewakottama?"

"No, Chief."

"It's Sanskrit and means serving the people above all. I hope this will explain my position in this matter. If you fax me photos of the criminal, it would be most helpful," said the burly, Arianto. He then thanked the detective for the courtesy call.

After Kelly's conversation with Chief Arianto, he placed his feet on his desk, lit a cigar, and grinned from ear to ear. He was aware that the Indonesian police had a reputation of being a highly corrupt force, but they were also brutal in exacting swift justice and were highly nationalistic. A foreigner, especially one with a criminal history, wouldn't be welcome. Making an example of such a man would serve notice to others who sought refuge from the authorities of their countries.

Billy was now in Chief Arianto's crosshairs.

Chapter 9

The Shakedown

I T WOULDN'T BE LONG before Chief Arianto visited the new American worker. He informed Billy of his conversation with Detective Kelly and said that under ordinary circumstances, he would have had the criminal jailed, never to be heard from again. But it was Billy's good fortune, the chief told him, that it was Indonesian Independence Day. The chief demanded half of Billy's weekly salary for his silence in the matter, then spit the extract of his cigar to the floor.

There was no alternative for the killer—either he agreed, or he would die in an Indonesian jail. Jeff Casey was now an investment for Arianto … with weekly returns.

Billy was barely settled in Indonesia, but he suspected if he stayed, sooner or later, Arianto would make impossible demands or make him disappear. Finding a way out of the country was not an easy task. The American oil company he worked for was his best chance of leaving, as it had tankers that distributed their product to several ports, including the United States. He believed no one would expect him to return to the country that wanted him the most, but he had a problem with the theory—Arianto. The moment Arianto discovered his investment had left the country, he'd call Detective Kelly.

Billy had to deal with the chief.

It was a hot August night, and he was to meet with Arianto for his weekly payment to the corrupt cop. The bearded chief, always came alone to the abandoned warehouse where they met, and today was no exception. It was seven thirty in the evening when Billy approached the chief's car. He always made his payment in a white envelope.

The chief never got out of his car when they met. He would lower his window on the driver's side, take the contribution, smile, and leave. Pleasantries were never exchanged. He expected tonight would be no different.

Arianto despised the man known to him as Jeff Casey, a common criminal with an alias who would be put to death if he were a citizen of Indonesia. But the chief didn't know he was dealing with a cold-blooded killer who was desperate.

The knife Billy held behind the envelope found its mark, slicing the throat of the chief, swiftly and effectively. The splatter of blood, blanketed most of the windshield, although some caught the killer's shirt. Billy judged that the chief's body wouldn't be found for days, which would give him the opportunity to leave the country before the authorities concluded he was the killer.

Arianto was a dirty cop, and such cops didn't brag where they found their extra revenue sources. The killer was sure it was safe to go back to the United States and finish the retribution process that tormented his daily thoughts. The element of surprise was always in his planning process. He knew Kelly had notified the Indonesian authorities, and he concluded that the detective supposed Billy's fate was sealed.

San Francisco

The American oil company granted Billy a bereavement leave, allowing him to be on the next tanker to the United States. He didn't have a grandmother, but the company granted the leave, as they needed another worker on the departing ship. It arrived in San Francisco in mid-September.

Billy was eating breakfast in a local diner when he overheard two college coeds discussing their summer break from school and saying they didn't look forward to the long drive back to Boston—his destination.

"Girls, I'm sorry to interrupt but I couldn't help overhearing that you're driving to Boston. I'm on my way to Quincy to attend my grandmother's funeral. My name is Jeff Casey and I'd like to propose driving back to the East Coast together and I'll pay all expenses."

Billy still had his charm and good looks. He was in his mid-thirties, but looked younger. He now sported a full head of recently dyed caramel-colored hair.

The girls were entering their senior year of college as twenty-year-olds. They asked if he could give them privacy to discuss his proposition. Billy took a seat at the counter.

"Gabby, we don't know this guy. It's an awfully long trip to take with a perfect stranger," said Emma.

"He seems harmless, but if you're that concerned, we'll ask for identification, take a cell phone picture of him and his license, and then send it to Claire with an explanation. Besides, he's willing to pay all of the expenses. I don't know about you, but I'm pretty tapped out."

The girls called over to Billy, who returned to their table. They discussed their concerns of going to Boston with a complete stranger. "But we'll go if you'll agree to our terms," Gabby said.

The killer had no safer alternative than traveling with the two students and he agreed to their conditions—he knew he'd have the opportunity to erase all evidence of being with the naive students. They took pictures of Billy and his license but failed to forward them to their friend.

The beginning day of the 3,000 mile journey was uneventful. Billy did all of the driving. They planned on spending five days on the road, driving 600 miles per day, stopping for food, and sleeping at motels.

The first evening, Emma and Gabby slept in the bed, and Billy on the couch. It was two o'clock in the morning when Emma bolted upright, waking from a dream. She looked toward the sofa; Billy was fast asleep, alleviating her concern that he was attacking her—her nightmare had seemed so real. The next day, they started the next segment of the journey.

Billy tried to get the coeds to lower their guard. "Say, you guys never told me what you're majoring in at school. Emma?"

The five-foot-five brunette was in good physical condition and very pretty. "I'm majoring in education. I expect to teach English in the Boston Public Schools system."

Gabby was taller at five-seven, with blonde hair, blue eyes, and also well proportioned. She was the more aggressive of the two and envisioned a close relationship with Billy before the completion of their journey. "So, Jeff, what do you do besides pick up girls and drive them to Boston?" she asked.

"I'm an oil rigger," he said.

"Is San Francisco where you work?" Emma asked.

"No, most of my work is in foreign countries."

"That must be exciting. Is there any one country you've enjoyed more than the others?" Gabby asked.

A competition between friends was developing, and Emma looked at Gabby with disdain.

"I would have to say … Thailand," he answered. "It's a wide-open country, and the people are very 'friendly,' if you know what I mean."

"Are the women any better than us?" Gabby asked.

Billy grinned. "Let's just say they're not afraid to show their wares."

The killer had their attention and would use it to make the long journey a pleasurable experience. They continued to discuss his experiences in different parts of the world and were intrigued with his carefully choreographed conversation, which led to a flirtation from the two coeds. They stopped at one of the plazas for lunch at one o'clock, ordering pizza and beers. As they were eating, two truckers stopped by their table. One whispered a comment, and the other laughed out loud.

Billy stood from his chair. "Can I help you men?"

"Yeah, we'd like a piece of this action. Seems like an awful lot of women for one man," said the bigger of the two men.

Without hesitation or warning, Billy grabbed the two bottles of beer on the table and swung them down on the heads of both men, causing each to fall to his knees. Billy followed with kicks to their heads. "Is that the action you were looking for?" he asked. Then he reached out for the girls' hands and hurried away from the plaza.

Billy's quick reaction stunned the two coeds, and as they fled the scene, they were breathless; they now idolized Billy. That evening, rather than compete for their new hero's affection, both immersed themselves in physical intimacy that fulfilled the killer's intent. The next day, with the relationship on a different level, the coeds were completely at ease. Conversation was no longer guarded but fluid and, at times, flirtatious. They were clueless that they were witnesses to the identity of a killer or that their lives were in peril.

Billy was seventy-two hours into the journey to Boston, and although the two coeds fulfilled his perverted indulgence, he had two days to speculate on disposal of the evidence. It had to be clean, as the girls were expected by family and friends. The killer calculated he had a window of three days after his arrival in Boston to deal with Savannah Moraine and flee the country. The question was, when and where could he dispose of the evidence?

This would be the final day of the coeds' journey.

Billy and the girls spent their last night in Columbus, Ohio, approximately 650 miles from Boston. The killer was noticeably quiet as he deliberated over when and how he would eliminate the two young women. He genuinely liked the girls and even had contemplated revealing his true identity. They were good company, and his travel would be less conspicuous with them along. It would be a risk, though—one with potentially dire consequences.

"Jeff, why so quiet?" Gabby asked.

"Just tired from the driving. The last part of a trip is always the most exhausting. We have at least twelve hours of travel ahead of us tomorrow."

"We can take turns driving, if that will help," Gabby said.

Emma nodded in agreement.

"Let's play it by ear," Billy said. "A good dinner and a soak in the tub will relieve the tension."

The three agreed to eat at a local steakhouse. Billy ordered a bottle of inexpensive champagne in celebration of their last night together. The girls had grown to like the handsome man they knew as Jeff. He was engaging and told interesting stories of his adventures in faraway lands, which elevated his stature in their eyes—they didn't know that most of his stories were fabricated. They were impressionable, as were most girls their age.

When they returned to the motel after dinner, Emma ran the water in the heart-shaped tub, and fifteen-minutes later, the three submerged themselves in the calming water, but not before Billy turned on the freestanding fan.

"Jeff, are you feeling better?" Emma asked. "You seemed to be somewhere else today."

"I've been preoccupied with the troubles that a friend of mine is having, and I don't know what advice to give him," the killer said.

"What's the issue?" Gabby asked.

Billy told of a young man who became a priest and used his trustworthiness to lure troubled women and boys into sexual relationships. And when his world was about to be exposed by his superior, he caused the prelate's death by faking an accident.

"He's killed others to hide his identity and has been on the run ever since," Billy said. "Then, he met a woman with whom he fell in love. She could identify him to the police if she ever saw one of the police photos distributed nationwide.

Now, he's faced with a conundrum: does he tell her of his past and risk future exposure … or eliminate the evidence?"

"When you say, *eliminate the evidence*, do you mean what I think it means?" Emma asked.

"Yes, kill the woman he's in love with. I really have mixed feelings on giving him any advice."

There was an eerie silence. *Is Jeff talking about another*, Gabby thought, *or is he … defining himself?* She glanced at Emma, who looked equally troubled, but neither one expressed their concerns.

Then came the moment that would determine the fate of the two coeds.

"So Emma, Gabby, what do I tell him?" Billy asked.

"Are you asking … if love conquers all, does she disregard the thought of sharing her bed with a killer? And will she feel threatened after any disagreements with him?" Gabby said.

"Is he prone to fits of explosive behavior, creating fear in her that she might be his next victim?" Emma asked.

"Love is a funny aphrodisiac," Gabby said. "Many sins are forgiven and even forgotten if the bond is unbreakable. Take Bonnie and Clyde, for example. Bonnie knew who Clyde was, yet she not only stayed with the killer but became part of his world. I think it depends on the person and how strong the desire is to be with her man."

"Are you that kind of person, Gabby?" the killer asked, drawing a line in the sand.

"Yeah, I think I am, Jeff."

"Well, I say, no way in hell!" Emma declared. "I'm not going to bed every night, not knowing if I'm going to be done in by some psycho."

"Hey, it's perfectly understandable to feel that way," Billy said. "I still don't know what to tell my friend, but what I do know is that I'm ready for a cold beer. Gabby, would you be an angel and get a round for us?"

The coed left the tub, her naked body dripping water along the way. Billy followed, emerging from the soapy water under the guise of having to relieve himself. When he stepped out, he stumbled into the fan, plunging it into the bathtub. Emma's body convulsed from the current, electrocuting the dissenting coed. Gabby screamed in horror and dropped the bottles of beer to the floor. The hideous sight and the odor of burning flesh was unbearable. She fainted and collapsed to the floor.

When Gabby regained consciousness, she was lying on the couch. Emma's lifeless body was still in the bathtub.

"Are you okay, Gabby?" Billy asked.

The shocked coed sat up, rotating her fingers against her temples. "Is Emma …?"

"I'm afraid so."

Gabby had seen Jeff stumble into the fan and sensed it had been a tragic accident. She asked if they should call 911 or the police, but the ex-priest rejected the idea.

"There will be too many questions, and my past …will cast suspicion on me."

Gabby stared at Jeff; her expression showed a worrisome awareness, and she suddenly feared she'd meet the same fate as Emma. She reached for Jeff's hands. She had to ask the question, even though she was apprehensive about hearing the answer. She hesitated, her mind calculating the words she was about to articulate. "Jeff, if the story you revealed about the friend seeking your advice was actually about you … I want you to know that I'm all in. You've touched me like no other man, and I don't want it to end." The coed hoped to convince the killer of her loyalty until she had a viable plan to escape from him.

It was up to Billy to determine his next move. Would Gabby be an asset in his travels, or would she bolt at the first opportunity?

When the morning sunrise signaled it was time for his departure, Billy removed all proof of his stay at the hotel. He secured both bodies in the trunk of the car and began the twelve-hour journey to Boston.

He was now responsible for the deaths of ten people … but there was more to do.

Chapter 10
The Unexpected

THE KILLER BURIED THE bodies at night on the property of a foreclosed farm in Lancaster, Pennsylvania. Gabby's killing troubled the ex-priest. Although she had given him the right answer, his compulsive personality kept whispering in his ear: *She'll have the past to use as a threat when your characters clash.*

As his hands tightened around Gabby's neck, her terrified expression elicited empathy from the killer and he loosened his grip on his intended victim. But then, as he wiped the perspiration from his eyes with the cuff of his shirt, his grip tightened until Gabby was dead. His schedule had now changed, and he waited until dark before leaving on the final leg of his journey.

The task of burying the two coeds' bodies didn't proceed without incident. Under the cover of darkness along an isolated side road on the farm, Billy was in the process of digging the grave when he heard laughter coming from where he had parked the car, some fifty-yards away. It was pitch-black, the overcast sky, blocking the moonlight. He quietly left the gravesite and proceeded toward his car. He noticed another car parked twenty-five feet from his, and two silhouettes appeared in the rear of the sport utility vehicle. Then the SUV bounced, apparently from the occupants' activity.

Billy commanded the two naked teenagers to leave the vehicle. The young girl pleaded for her life after witnessing the bludgeoning death of her companion. One blow from the shovel to her head rendered her unconscious. Billy dragged both bodies to the partially dug gravesite and continued the task of burying his victims.

When he completed the grizzly work, he drove the victims' vehicle a quarter mile from his own, placed a rag in the gas cap opening and set it on fire. He returned to the gravesite of the four bodies. He then cut a large limb from a tree and dragged the ground from the site to his car, discarding the branch just before reaching the main road. The loud explosion of the SUV shook the ground and lit up the night sky as Billy made a hasty retreat.

The two teens were reported missing by their parents. The local police were baffled and had no clues to their disappearance. The two had no history of civil disobedience with authorities and were popular with their classmates. Special cadaver-trained dogs were utilized to detect blood and human remains, but the authorities were searching where the teens' SUV was found. It wasn't until a day later that a deputy speculated that perhaps their search was too narrow in scope.

They expanded their operation to twenty-five yard grids. Then, one of the dogs started to yelp. Sticking out from the ground was a plastic straw. All three dogs now barked at the location. A police captain yelled for a deputy to bring a shovel. It was a shallow gravesite, and within minutes of digging, they were stunned by what they discovered. The missing female teen was lying on top of three other bodies with a plastic straw in her mouth, which provided the air for her to survive the ordeal; the young girl regained consciousness and had the presence of mind to reach for the discarded straw while the killer was digging her grave. The terrorized teen moved her fingers, clutching to her only hope of survival, taking shallow breaths, always in fear of discovery.

The thrown soil splattered on her face. She was being buried alive, the killer, unaware of the teens extraordinary will to live. If she moved too soon, she would be bludgeoned to death. When she could no longer hold her breath, the straw slowly broke through the shallow grave.

Rebecca Arlin had been struck in the head with a shovel, but the killer never confirmed she was dead. The high school swimming champion was rushed to the local hospital, a witness to the killer's identity.

The coroner took Emma's and Gabby's bodies to the morgue for identification and to determine cause of death, but the authorities now had a living witness in Rebecca to help identify the killer of her boyfriend and the two coeds. She was the daughter of a prominent family in the community and would command special attention by the Lancaster Police Department.

Billy showed no remorse in killing the teens; they were collateral damage, and his soul had turned dark. The ex-priest wasn't considered a mass murderer or a serial killer by the strict definition of the terms, but he was a killer with revenge in his heart and had no reservations about those who stood in his way. He took no souvenirs from his victims, as serial killers often did, nor were his victims in one specific location, as when mass killings occur. He was just a man who was so blinded by revenge and hatred that reality was nonexistent.

Billy was on his way to Boston, and based upon his plan, he had only two days to complete the killing of Savannah Moraine. He didn't check into a hotel when reaching Boston, fearing he would be exposed. Instead, he abandoned Emma's car and stole another. He changed the license plates from the stolen car with those taken from a third vehicle, and then he spent the remaining night under an old viaduct.

The next morning, he called the hotel that was the last known address of Savannah Moraine. He told the receptionist that he was Detective Kelly of the Boston Police Department, after which the receptionist provided Billy with all the information he needed to locate his target. Savannah had moved her business location to another upscale hotel.

Kelly continued to have recurring nightmares since the murder of his partner four years earlier. His bedroom was a constant reminder of the intimacies he'd shared with Maggie. His heart was broken; his soul mate was gone. Every item in the apartment was a memory of a lost love. The escape of her killer haunted him daily, and his only consolation was the knowledge that the ex-priest's fate was in the hands of the corrupt Indonesian police—or so he thought.

Mike was sitting at his desk at ten o'clock in the morning, reviewing the national and local police reports. The killing of the college coeds, Rebecca's boyfriend and her survival, made national headlines and the morning newscast. The detective's curiosity was stirred. He called the Indonesian Police Department, hoping that the twelve-hour time difference would still give rise to a response. When he heard a voice on the other end, he asked to speak to Chief Tito Arianto.

The Boston detective was shaken when he was informed that the chief had been murdered. Kelly's instincts kicked in, and he immediately called the Lancaster Police Department. He asked to speak to the officer in charge of the Rebecca Arlin case. He asked the detective about the facts and the other bodies found. The two coeds were identified as Emma Long and Gabby Stone, both from Boston.

Mike asked the detective to repeat the names again, and when he did, Kelly was aghast. When Maggie Burns was murdered, Mike had been assigned another partner, Nick Stone, a twenty-five year veteran of the police force—and the father of Gabby.

Kelly left his desk and stopped at the water cooler. After drinking, he saw Stone walking toward him. He didn't know if his partner had been informed that his daughter had been murdered.

"Hi, Mike, what's on our agenda today?" Nick asked.

Kelly slowly rubbed his forehead. *How do you tell a person that his only child has been brutally murdered and discarded like garbage in a shallow grave?* He took a deep breath and said, "Sit down for minute, Nick."

"Mike, what is it? Spit it out, partner."

When Kelly informed Stone what had happened to his daughter, the detective stood in disbelief. "There must be a mistake," he whispered.

When Mike asked if Gabby was traveling with another friend, Stone slammed both hands to the desk, his worst fear verified. The facts of the case were incomplete, and Kelly had little to tell his partner. His concern for the killing of the Indonesian police chief was pushed aside for the moment, as his partner's grief was in the forefront.

It was almost eleven o'clock when Kelly called the Lancaster Police Department. He informed the detective in charge of Gabby's case, that she was the daughter of his partner. There was silence on the other end; the men in blue took exception to the killing of one of their own or a member of a cop's family.

The initial report from the coroner was that Gabby Stone had been strangled to death, but something else was revealed: the coroner believed that Gabby had known her killer.

"The initial strangulation didn't kill her," the coroner said. "Death was from a second strangulation point applied to her neck."

Mike asked his partner if Gabby had mentioned anyone accompanying her and her friend from San Francisco.

"There was no conversation with my daughter suggesting that another person *was* traveling with them. But Gabby wouldn't have told me anyway; she'd have known I would insist it was a bad idea. She had a will of her own and was a bit testy at times, like most her age. But I wouldn't be surprised if she went ahead and took on another passenger. Now, I have to break the news to her mother and Gabby's stepfather."

"Do you want company?"

Nick shook his head dejectedly. "No, Mike, this isn't going to be pleasant. Caitlin didn't want Gabby to make this trip to San Francisco, but I told her that the kid had to grow up and spread her wings a bit."

Stone knocked on the front door of his ex-wife's home. When she answered and saw the expression on his face, she knew something was awry—he never just appeared.

"Honey, who is it?" Caitlin's husband asked as he came to the front door. He placed his arm around his wife, saying, "Nick, what's going on?"

"It's Gabby. There's been …" Nick couldn't go on. He covered his face with his hands and wept. In his line of work, he had notified next of kin when a family member died, but this was different; it was his daughter.

Caitlin cupped her hands to her face, praying that what she expected to hear wasn't true, even as she had a sinking feeling that her only child had died. "God, no, oh, God! Not my baby. This isn't happening!" she wailed, bracing for the grisly details.

When Nick told her, his ex-wife shrieked loudly and fell to her knees. It was too early to place blame on her ex-husband for allowing their daughter to make the trip to San Francisco. It was time to mourn and time to find her killer. Gabby's body wouldn't be released until the coroner had completed the autopsy. It would be several days before the Lancaster police released the body to her parents. Her cell phone and the photo of Billy and his license would still be intact.

Nick retuned to the precinct and was greeted by the detectives in his squad, all giving their condolences and offering to help capture the man who had murdered his daughter. The captain called Nick into his office and offered his sympathy to the detective. He suggested Stone take a month of bereavement time to settle his affairs, which he rejected.

"Thanks, Captain, but keeping busy is what I need now—and finding the bastard who killed my girl."

"The case is in the hands of the Lancaster Police Department, and their chief of police has assured us of a full court press to find your daughter's killer. I've offered any assistance he needs, but you know the routine, Nick. Department rules mandate that you can't be involved in the investigation. I don't want to hear complaints from Lancaster about a rogue cop from Boston interfering in their investigation. Everybody out there has your back, but they'll be told the same thing I just said to you—this case is not in our jurisdiction. Are we clear?"

"We're clear, Captain."

Both men were unaware that Mike Kelly held a thread that linked the case of Gabby Stone to other murders in Boston.

Nick returned to his desk. Mike sat across from him, on the telephone with the Lancaster police. When he completed the call, he began the process of finding the killer. He had to ask tough questions, and Nick understood.

Mike asked his partner if he knew which credit cards Gabby had used. He didn't, but he said his ex-wife would have that information. He didn't make the call; it was Mike, in his official capacity as a detective with the Boston Police Department. This also avoided potential outrage by Nick's ex-wife if he made the call.

Kelly then called the credit card companies provided by Caitlin Stone, but it proved a dead end. There was no record of her cards being used after she left San Francisco—the killer had paid cash for motels, gas, and food.

The two detectives plotted the route that the girls would have traveled from San Francisco to Boston, jotting down all possible motels, lodges, and hotels along I-80 East, as well as all toll booths. They divided the list, each calling the locations and giving the descriptions of Emma and Gabby. Nick was the first to get a hit, and Mike got one shortly thereafter. In each case, the name *Jeff Casey* was on the registration.

When Mike heard the description of Casey, he was stunned. The ex-priest had left his footprint on the murder of his partner's daughter.

Kelly's phone rang; it was the Lancaster detective working the murder of Gabby Stone. They had found a cell phone that was buried with the coed and forwarded the photos to the Boston detective. One of the photos was of a man, and another was of his driver's license. When the Lancaster detective checked the central base of the motor vehicles files, the man in the photo didn't fit the description on the license. He was faxing the information to Kelly to see if he or Gabby's father could identify the man.

Mike hurried to the fax machine and waited anxiously to receive the photos. When he did, the Boston detective was stunned.

"Son of a bitch! I don't believe it!" Mike barked, sitting back in his chair.

"What is it, Mike?" His partner put his phone down, anxious for an explanation.

"Your daughter just spoke to us, Nick. Gabby snapped a picture of the man who was with her and Emma on their way home from San Francisco."

Mike recounted the story of Father Billy Pratt, the killer ex-priest. His partner was speechless as the tale of the murderer unfolded. Mike suddenly stopped his story, and the expression on his face was that of alarm.

"What, Mike?" Stone asked.

Mike didn't respond. Instead, he grabbed his phone, dialed, and waited for someone to answer. When no one did, Kelly slammed the phone down and said, "Come with me. We're leaving immediately. Pratt must be back in town to kill the woman responsible for bringing him down, Savannah Moraine."

They drove to her last known address; Kelly was the only one privy to her location. They ran up to the second floor of the apartment complex, but when they approached Savannah's flat, they noticed the door was ajar. Both reached for their weapons. They entered the apartment cautiously, each covering the other's back.

The complex was empty. Kelly took a deep breath and exhaled slowly—there wasn't a body. But his relief would be short-lived. He noticed a piece of tattered material clinging to a closed window in the bedroom. He opened the double hung window and leaned out, and then immediately slammed both hands on the frame. In the courtyard of the complex was a woman's body.

He was too late. The killer had gotten to Savannah.

Kelly had underestimated the determination and prowess of the disgraced priest. This killer was a man of patience, letting years pass before reappearing—waiting until it was totally unexpected from the former cleric.

The detective now was certain that Pratt was responsible for the death of his partner and Savannah Moraine. Never in his career had he been challenged by a criminal with Billy's tenacity and daring. He was going to need help in order to capture the ex-priest and end his senseless and murderous actions. The hunt would intensify.

Chapter 11
The Hunt

T HE CHIEF OF DETECTIVES held a meeting the day after the murder of Savannah Moraine. He gave a profile of Billy John Pratt and said he was a person of interest, a suspect in the recent killing of Gabby Stone, and a confidential informant. He also indicated that Pratt was a person of interest in several other murders, including one of their own.

"Gentlemen, this is really a bad guy, suspected of additional homicides in Venezuela and Indonesia. He cannot be underestimated, and if cornered, he will not hesitate to kill his pursuers. We've informed Interpol and put out an all-states bulletin of his description. All transportation venues—air, rail, and bus terminals—have been given a forensic description of the killer, copies of which will be distributed to each of you at the end this meeting. This guy has killed one of our own; he's a high-priority target. Check with your informants, and be generous with your promises. It's boots on the pavement, gentlemen. Let's get this scumbag, dead or alive!"

The chief's statement on apprehending Billy was indicative of the intense atmosphere in the squad room. Most often, the capturing of a known criminal was by the book—arrest the felon alive, whenever possible, so motive could be established and possible co-conspirators named. But if your life is threatened when attempting to place the criminal into custody, the use of deadly force is warranted. The chief was giving a clear message: take Pratt down.

Billy's escape was not going to be easy, considering the nature of his crime and the intense dragnet placed on all routes out of the state. But the killer ex-priest had a plan and had anticipated the police tightening all lines of transportation out of Boston and Massachusetts. He concluded a nationwide alert would be posted, and Interpol would be notified.

Billy's route was an ingenious plan of action, but it was also humbling, as he'd have to traverse the rat-infested sewer system of Boston. He had plotted a map that would begin at Savannah Moraine's street and end at one of Boston's largest car dealerships. Under the darkness of night, he would leave the sewer, replacing the manhole cover, and climb on top of a car-carrier trailer, one that left every week on the same day. He entered one of the several vehicles the semitrailer was to deliver to the Bayonne Port of New Jersey. The cars would then be stored in containers for their eventual destination to Rio de Janeiro. Under the pretense of a worker on the dock, he would remain on the ship and work as a crew member. He'd never be challenged, as many cargo ships frequently changed personnel on every consignment delivered to a foreign country.

Several days had passed, and the Boston police were stymied. They choked off all routes out of the city and state yet were mystified that their efforts were unproductive. Pratt seemed to have vanished into thin air. It was particularly frustrating for Nick Stone, and the scene at his daughter's burial was particularly distressing.

After the young coed was laid to rest, Caitlin Stone turned to her ex-husband, crying, "It's all your fault! She's dead because of you, you naive bastard. Let her spread her wings, you said. Let her spread her wings! Are you happy? You killed her!" With that, Caitlin collapsed next to her daughter's grave.

"How does an ex-priest escape when every cop on the planet is looking for him?" Nick Stone, later asked Mike.

"When my ex-partner and I interviewed him after three priests fell to their deaths from the second-floor balcony of the church, he confessed to being an avid reader of books about killers. He wanted to know what made a person take the extreme step of taking a person's life," Mike said.

"We have to get this guy. I won't rest until we track him down," Nick snarled. "Then, I want five minutes alone with this mutt."

Mike didn't have a response for the man whose daughter had been brutally killed and buried in a shallow grave with three other victims.

Two weeks had passed, and the police were no closer to capturing the ex-priest.

The man seemed to have vanished; his studying the criminal world served him well. There were several sightings of the elusive killer, but all proved futile. Sifting through the hundreds of callers who claimed to have seen the killer was a tedious undertaking; many were seeking to collect the $500,000 reward posted by the FBI. Billy John Pratt was now on the Ten Most Wanted Fugitives list.

But no one wanted to capture the man more than Nick Stone. The six-foot two, two-hundred-pound detective wallowed in the memories of his daughter. His marriage had been destroyed by the job, the irregular hours and the days away from home, but he always found time for his little girl, whom he affectionately called, Cupcake.

Nick turned the pages of his scrapbook while sipping whiskey and smiling at the images of his daughter; he remembered events as though they were yesterday. One photo in particular raised the stakes of his emotions—Gabby, as a precocious four year old, holding up a cupcake before leaving for preschool. He remembered she'd asked, "Daddy, why did you and Mommy name me Gabby, and why do you call me, Cupcake?"

"When you were born, Cupcake, you made such a fuss in the nursery. The doctor called you a gabby little baby when he informed me you'd been born and that Mommy was okay. So your mother and I thought that would be the perfect name for you. Now, why do I call you, Cupcake? Because when I kiss your cheeks, they taste just as sweet as a cupcake." The little girl had giggled and hugged her daddy.

The recollection was too painful for the Boston detective. He threw his glass against the wall, weeping for the lost treasure of his life. His rage for his daughter's killer was without limits. Now, the only purpose of his existence was to capture, torture, and feed the dismembered body of the ex-priest to the rats of the sewer from which he'd come. He continued to lament the loss of his daughter until the excess of alcohol rendered him unconscious.

Three Years Later

"Montes, get that truck ready to go in five minutes," demanded the man who headed the group of poachers.

Billy was now in Brazil and using the alias, Diego Montes.

Poaching was a quick way of making serious money, although the high return was due to the ever-present danger of being shot or jailed for those willing to step over the line of the law. The Javari Valley of Brazil was a fertile field for poachers of gold mines, protected species of fish and turtles. The more adventurous worked for cocaine smugglers, using the Solimoes River and trekking through the deep jungle, where anacondas, alligators, and poison dart frogs lurked along the way.

For the ex-priest, the danger was no more perilous than the possibility of being captured by Interpol or the FBI. When the killer determined that the funds he'd accumulated were enough to live comfortably, the lure of Rio de Janeiro and its annual decadent celebration of Carnival, was the aphrodisiac that accommodated his insatiable sexual appetite.

Billy rented a modest apartment in Rio, but the irony was that his balcony faced the iconic Christ the Redeemer statue on the summit of Corcovado. The daily image of the sculpture was a haunting reminder of his past sins, and after six months, the ex-priest fled to Sao Paulo, the largest city in Brazil. It was on the east coast and was a focal point for commerce. He escaped the repetition of daily life in Rio de Janeiro, as well as possible exposure to the police or recognition by one of the thousands of tourists who visited the city. He had taken a chance by escaping to Brazil, a country with an extradition treaty with the United States. The ex-priest reasoned that the authorities would be looking for him in countries without extradition treaties, which had been his rationalization for his brief stay in Venezuela and Indonesia.

Diego Montes bought into a partnership with a cattle rancher; the spread was located on the outskirts of Sao Paulo. After a year of working together, both agreed that if one or the other died, the spread would belong to the survivor. The seventy-five-year-old rancher had no children and was looking for a younger partner to carry on the business. Billy, now forty, was the perfect fit for the bronze-face Brazilian, and the relationship developed into a father-son kinship.

Alec D'Souza was born in Brazil. At age sixteen, he was working on a large cattle ranch. At the age of thirty, he was made foreman and continued in that position for twenty-five years. He was well regarded by his patron and was grateful to the man who had saved his child from certain death by a giant anaconda. The boy had fallen asleep under a large tree near the river. The sixteen-foot snake curled itself around the six year old, tightening its muscles until the boy was near death. Alec came upon the scene and used his machete to dislodge the boy from the snake. He then hacked the snake's head from the rest of the body. His patron showed his gratitude by gifting Alec, 100 acres of land and fifty-head of cattle to start his own business, with the stipulation that he wouldn't expand unless agreed upon by the larger ranches in the valley.

Each cow needed up to two acres of grazing land. In order for D'Souza to enlarge his business, he would have to purchase more land. He explained the agreement to Billy and pointed out his responsibility to abide by the arrangement. He anticipated that he would die before Billy.

"Diego, I'm aware that you're not a native Brazilian, but no one will question your heritage, even if they think you're running away from your past. What's important to the patrons is that you're a man of principle, a man who keeps his word. Their *fazendas*, or what you know as a ranch, are their lives. Most fazendas have been in their families for generations and many of their gaucho ranch hands were born where they work."

Billy appreciated the man's profound sincerity. Now he was not only his patron in partnership but in a spirituality that touched the remaining dignity of the ex-priest. Alec shared his insightfulness with genuine concern, as a father would to a son; this was something lost by the man who had killed twelve people.

"Alec, I want you to know how much I appreciate your wisdom and guidance. It's very special. I wish we could have met some years ago," said Billy, suddenly guilt-ridden.

"Diego, the Bible makes reference to Jesus intervening when a crowd gathered to stone a woman for her infidelity," Alec said.

"Yes, and Jesus said, 'He who is without sin, cast the first stone.'"

During their lengthy conversations, the Brazilian rancher suspected that his protege was once in a religious order because of his knowledge of the scriptures and the ministerial tone he used at times, which reminded the rancher of his religious teachings as a boy when he attended Sunday church services. He never asked Billy to verify or deny his suspicions; he respected Billy's privacy and imagined he might be fleeing from personal demons.

Within sixteen months of their partnership, Alec D'Souza died. Billy was now the owner of the cattle ranch. Several of the local ranchers attended the services of Alec, whom they fondly called AD.

Billy didn't take the death of his patron well, and he tried to console himself by consuming numerous caipirinhas, made of hard liquor, sugar, and lime. The man who showed no remorse in the vengeful killings of those who could expose him, lay pitifully on the floor of the house he had shared with Alec. His binge lasted for days and was interrupted only when one of the local ranchers sent his daughter with a basket of food to his house. She knocked on the door of the modest home but there was no response. The thirty-year old woman peeked in a window and saw Billy on the floor. Afraid that something had happened to the man known as Diego Montes, she dashed home and told her father what she had seen.

Gabino Santos owned the largest ranch in the valley; his cattle farm abutted Billy's. He was the son of Alec's patron, the man AD had worked for most of his life and the boy he had saved from the constrictions of a deadly anaconda. He arrived at Billy's home with two of his men, who carried the ex-priest to a horse-drawn carriage. The next morning, the process of sobering him up began—first by soaking in a bath and then by eating a breakfast of French bread, white cheese, dark coffee, and papaya.

"Mr. Montes, some more coffee?" asked Gabrielle, the patron's daughter.

"Please," responded the thankful Billy. The devils in his head still were swinging their picks.

"How are you feeling, Diego?" Gabino Santos asked.

"A lesson learned, patron," Billy responded.

Gabino smiled and then asked his daughter to fetch three aspirins.

Gabrielle was a very attractive woman. She was brown-skinned with brown eyes and dark hair and stood a slender five-five. She had married at the age of twenty-five and was widowed by twenty-nine; her husband was gored by the bull on the ranch. Her father shot the animal and ordered his men to feed the carcass to the piranhas in a nearby river. There were no children in the marriage, much to the disappointment of her parents, as she and her husband had planned to not have children for five years.

Gabrielle returned with the aspirin, Billy, eyeballing the rancher's daughter as she handed him the medication.

"Mr. Montes, would you honor us by having dinner with us this evening?" Isubela Santos asked.

Billy accepted the invitation; he wanted to be with others during his period of mourning and wished to know the host's daughter on a more personal basis.

Over dinner, Gabino asked, "Diego, how did you and Alec make each other's acquaintance?"

"I was interested in cattle ranching, and he was looking for a financial partner. We seemed to be the right fit from the beginning, first as partners, and then … he became a dear friend and mentor," Billy said with a heavy heart.

It was clear Billy was grief-stricken, so the patron redirected the somber conversation. "Diego, it's not every day that a stranger comes into our valley and becomes part of our social order. What brought you to Sao Paulo? It's not Rio de Janeiro, although we're part of the biggest municipality in Brazil."

If Billy coveted life in what he carefully weighed as a perfect refuge from his past, he needed to secure the trust of the Santos family. He had to unfold the layers of his past, while seemingly answering the question. He had to convey self-assurance to this family—his neighbors and the girl he intended to become his wife. Such a marriage would give him validation with the Santos and the other influential ranchers.

The killer of twelve explained to Gabino that he was an orphan, raised by the Sisters of Charity. When he attained legal adulthood, the sisters forced him to enter the seminary to become a priest.

With this revelation, Isubela Santos made the sign of the cross and looked at her husband.

The ex-priest continued to paint a picture of torment and uncertainty in his life. He said that when he was ordained and then assigned pastoral duties, he questioned his commitment and finally decided to run from the demons torturing his soul. The Santos family was captivated by Billy's story; the mother made the sign of the cross several times as he spoke.

"But what about the years after you fled the priesthood?" Gabino asked.

"There were many journeys over time, some of which I'm not proud to mention, but some were enriching experiences. What I'm about to reveal will not endear me to you, but it's necessary, for if you learned of it from someone else, I fear I'd lose your trust and friendship. I worked for a man who was the leader of poachers. We stole from the earth and from nature. I must admit it was the darkest part of my life. I was guilt-ridden and decided to turn my life around, so I sought good in my life. That's when I met Alec; he was my gift from the man above, a sign that I was forgiven for disavowing my unchosen vocation. All I seek is peace. I want to build roots in something I believe in, and I hope that can be here in the valley."

The Santos' were moved by the passion in Billy's narrative. After dinner, their guest craftily shifted the conversation, asking about the history of the Santos family, which was warmly accepted and expounded upon by the patron. At the end of the evening, Billy thanked the Santos' and was about to leave for his ranch when Mrs. Santos insisted he stay the night. Her agenda wasn't clear at the time, but what better potential husband for her daughter than a former priest?

The next morning, Gabino summoned his foreman to take Billy home in the horse-drawn carriage. Galtero Gomes was forty-two; a dark-skinned man who stood six-feet tall—taller than the average Brazilian—and weighed a brawny 200 pounds. He had been working on the Santos ranch since he was fifteen, following in the tradition of Santos's father when he made Alec D'Souza the foreman of the ranch. Billy was unaware that Galtero had his sights set on marrying Gabrielle.

"So gringo, what brings you to the valley?" asked the muscular foreman, spitting the extract from his cigar.

Billy heard the disdain in his tone and immediately saw the foreman as a threat—and this triggered a return to his primal instinct of survival.

Billy didn't subscribe to the idea of making friends with your adversary; on the contrary, his history proved his intent was to dispose of the menace. He humored himself by telling the foreman that he was running from a relationship with an overbearing male partner.

The foreman's immediate reaction was to move farther away from Billy and then spit the cigar from his mouth. There was some comfort in the ex-priest's response; the Santos' foreman thought that if Billy was gay, he'd have no designs on Gabrielle.

For Billy, the foreman's comfort would make his task uncomplicated.

Chapter 12

The Butterfly

THE SWEET NECTAR DEVOURED by the butterfly was Billy's challenge in his pursuit of Gabrielle Santos. He had to provide an aphrodisiac for the unsuspecting woman, who was still mourning her late husband, who had passed the previous year. He sent her Ernest Hemingway's *Farewell to Arms* as a thank-you for her kindness in his hour of need. It was a book he could relate to; it depicted desertion, love, pain, and loyalty. Alec had given it to him.

Two days after receiving the gift, she invited Billy to dinner at her home, after receiving permission from her parents. It was time for Billy to transform from his former self to that of a doting pursuer. The stares across the table were conspicuous and metamorphic for the ex-priest. He was in an aquarium of curiosity. Gabrielle's mother was waiting to scoop him within her net and declare her daughter's mourning at an end.

After dinner, Billy and Gabrielle left the dining room for the expansive porch overlooking the immense holdings of her family. The sun was setting below the horizon, painting a regal portrait of the beautiful countryside. They exchanged thoughts and the revealing, heart-to-heart dialogue reserved for those beyond the realm of acquaintance. Like the four-winged butterfly unmasking its brilliant colors, Billy parroted the dance of a lover; he endeavored to trigger the pheromones of Gabrielle. He entertained her with the parodies of a priest and compared the vow of celibacy to a woman living without shoes, pocketbooks, or mirrors. They both laughed at the metaphor and at times giggled. His approach took hold as they traveled to his ranch. She asked him to show her the books he had accumulated in the home he'd shared with Alec, which was now his own, and the materials provided a glimpse into the man she found more and more interesting. As they walked past the workers' bunkhouse, the foreman of the Santos ranch sat with his legs folded on the top railing. He smacked his lips in mockery of the passing outlander and then barked out, "Gabrielle, why are you wasting time with this gringo homosexual?"

Infuriated, Gabrielle responded, "Galtero, would you like your patron informed that you disrespected his guest?"

Billy tugged at her hand, urging her to ignore the man he intended to kill. When they arrived at the front door of Billy's home, he placed his hands on her waist. Her silhouette shimmered against the full moon of the evening, and their lips met. Their passions were provoked. Their longing bodies crossed the boundaries of conventional propriety. There was no innocence or bashful pretense or discreetness in their cravings; it was simply heated frenzy.

"It's eleven o'clock, Isubela, and our daughter is still not in her bed," Gabino said.

"Gabino, I know you're concerned, but she's a thirty-year old woman who has been without the warmth and comfort of a man for too long. Give her some room to once again experience love," said his wife as she lovingly placed her hand to his face, providing solace. They embraced and then retired for the evening.

The next morning, Gabrielle joined her parents for breakfast. A servant poured coffee into her cup. She was radiant, and her smile was the chronicle of the previous evening's gratification.

"You're beaming this morning, my daughter," Gabino said, sipping on his coffee and peering at his wife.

"Yes, my father; it's a wonderful morning," said Gabrielle, stretching her hands high above her head.

"And your plans for the day?" he asked.

"Diego has invited me to lunch, and I accepted, if that meets with your approval, Father."

Her mother placed her hand on her husband's in a silent appeal for tolerance.

"Gabrielle, you're the precious jewel of our treasure, and we only desire our daughter's contentment and happiness. Embrace the wisdom of the turtle, my dear, and not the brashness of the rabbit."

"Father, what you and Mama have taught me through the years was to follow my heart with my *cabesa*," Gabrielle said, pointing to her head. She bit down on her toast, gulped a mouthful of coffee, and then hugged her father and kissed his cheek. She embraced her mother and then dashed away to shower and prepare for the day's adventure with her newfound lover.

"This new kind of behavior is very strange to me, Mama Santos," Gabino said.

"Gabino, it's 2002, not the world of your father and mine. Do you recollect our adventurous ways, my husband? If my father knew when you deflowered his daughter, you would have joined the bull you shot for goring Ignacio," Isubela said. Her husband's devilish smile showed he was celebrating the memory.

They were both nineteen when they married, and a year later, Gabriella was born—their parents had counted the months from the blessed event.

"I see the fifty-one-year-old cabesa still remembers my sexy body," his wife said.

"Isubela, you're still the most beautiful woman in my eyes. Your marvelous body produced a beautiful child. I don't want her hurt. I'll have a talk with Diego and express our concerns."

"Be sympathetic, Gabino," urged his wife.

Isubela was the daughter of a prominent cattle rancher in the valley. Her parents and Gabino's were tragically killed when their plane crashed on its way to Alentejo, Portugal. It was the birthplace of their fathers and mothers, who had raised Mertolenga cattle before moving to Brazil.

Isubela was a very attractive woman at five-foot four and a mirror image of her daughter. Her husband was a portly five-eight and sported a pencil-thin mustache. Both parents were brown-skinned but lighter than most Brazilians.

It was a balmy June day; the temperatures of the seacoast towns were rarely above eighty degrees and generally in the seventies. Billy and Gabrielle were enjoying a picnic lunch under a small tree, where the aroma of tropical flowers attracted a variety of butterflies. Their month-long romance had intensified. Billy assured Gabino Santos that his intentions were honorable, and her father gave his blessing for Billy to continue courting his daughter.

The ex-priest had found something he hadn't experienced in the past—a feeling of belonging to something of value, the treasure of true love. With the butterflies surrounding the flowers, it was an enchanting time for Billy and an aberrational transformation. When a butterfly landed on his hand, he raised it above his shoulder, and the insect spread its wings, exposing its captivating colors. Billy was mesmerized by the creature; he experienced a reverence he hadn't felt while serving his God. The world around him seemed to crystalize into one of romance and perceptiveness, and he no longer felt the need for retribution against those he thought had betrayed him.

Was it possible for this killer of twelve souls to rise from his inner demons and be reborn into a world of beauty and reconciliation? Could he approach an adversary like Galtero Gomes while conducting himself with civility? Could he unburden himself of his alternative response of the past? He would be tested within moments, as an abrupt pain penetrated his chest.

Billy had been shot, and blood splattered across Gabrielle's white blouse. Her scream sent the butterflies aloft, and she called her father on her cell phone, hysterically recounting what had happened, while remembering her late husband's death.

Billy was taken to the hospital and underwent life-threatening surgery. Those concerned waited for word on the success or failure of the seven-hour operation. When the surgeon appeared, he said that the next twenty-four hours would determine the outcome for the man who had stolen their hearts.

Would God take revenge on the fallen priest, the ex-ambassador of faith?

Three weeks passed, and Billy was convalescing at the Santos hacienda; he'd been given a door of redemption. Gabrielle was by his side throughout the horrific experience. Her father was outraged that Diego's life had been threatened on his hacienda. Those who lived in the valley had their own justice system, having fought off poachers and thieves for years.

Gabino Santos suspected the attempted killing was due to jealousy or retribution. When he discovered that it was Galtero who attempted to kill Billy, it was an affront to Gabino's trust. He met with the valley's court of justice, the Tribunal Cinco, which consisted of the ranchers from the five biggest cattle farms in Sao Paulo. Santos presented his case, and the verdict was immediate.

Galtero's body would disappear; it would be fed to the piranha-infested waters of the nearby river. Those who worked with the foreman understood the penalty for his transgression. Within two months of the Galtero's disappearance, Gabino asked Billy if he would consider becoming the new supervisor of his ranch. His future father-in-law had his men tend to Billy's spread during his convalescence. Billy accepted the offer and the two discussed merging the ranches, as the patron indicated his daughter would be the benefactor of the combined ranches in the future.

The wedding between Billy and Gabrielle was planned for September and would be held at the Santos hacienda. In a private discussion between Gabino and his future son-in-law, the father of the bride explained that a mandated prenuptial agreement must be signed. The Tribunal Cinco banned non-native individuals from ownership of property in the valley. It was a private shareholders agreement among the five ranchers, who could sell to other members or leave their holdings to a family member but never to an outsider.

Gabrielle would become Billy's patroness, and Billy found that acceptable, considering he was in transition and cultivating a sense of grounding. Giving the members of the Tribunal Cinco community details of the groom's background was non-compulsory, as respecting privacy was a tenet of the group.

The marriage ceremony was performed in Sao Paulo's cathedral, the most prominent Catholic church in Brazil. It was a troubling experience for Billy as he glanced at the cross while battling past demons. The sacrament of marriage asked God for his blessing in the union between Billy and Gabrielle, while excommunicated from his church when his transgression with Savannah Moraine was discovered. He began to perspire, and his heart beat faster. He hallucinated that angels of death were circling above him. When the host was about to be administered, he was overcome with anxiety, fearful he would be punished for receiving holy communion.

"Diego, are you okay?" asked Gabrielle, when Billy didn't respond to the clergyman's question of consent.

"Sorry, Father, of course I do."

When the exchange of consent was completed by the bride—now Mrs. Gabrielle Santos Montes—the host was administered to both bride and groom. The blessed wafer singed the tongue of the ex-priest, and he feared if he swallowed it, he would be disemboweled by the souls of his victims, awaiting revenge.

He waited for the retribution, but it hid in his subconscious.

One hundred fifty guests attended the wedding celebration. It was an outdoor affair on the grounds of the hacienda and challenged the grand ballrooms of the prestigious hotels in San Paulo. The food was plentiful; the music was elegant and fashionable. Billy and his future bride discussed at length their plans for the honeymoon.

Two Weeks Prior

"Diego, Paris is the city I've always dreamed of visiting. It would be a wonderful honeymoon," said the future bride.

Billy's silence was telling. Could he trust her response to the truth? How could he enlighten Gabrielle about his past without her anger forcing him to flee the country? He had to assemble a believable story and at the same time, be sympathetic.

"When I was a priest," he told Gabrielle, "I heard the confession of an individual who admitted to killing several people; he was a hired gunman with worldwide affiliations. When the police approached me regarding the killer, I couldn't say anything; I was bound by the ecclesiastical law of confidentiality between a priest and a confessor. That was a time when I struggled with my vows of being a priest because the killer was a menace to society. I knew my guilt and remorse would be devastating if the killer struck again, and I'd had the power to prevent such acts.

"So I cooperated with the authorities after leaving the priesthood, and I testified to the killer's revelations. I realized that by testifying against the killer, my own life would be in jeopardy, but I felt saving other potential victims was more important. After receiving several death threats, I decided it was time to leave the country, I thought Sao Paulo was so remote that no one would find me." He sighed heavily. "So I am a hunted man, which prevents me from going anywhere that requires a passport. I'm so sorry, my love. I didn't intend for my problems to interfere with your passion for Paris."

Billy's narrative was brilliant and convincing, yet unfulfilling. Something was flawed within it, and the guilt he experienced was perplexing. His inner torment was disturbing and was a disconnect from his narcissistic past.

Then, the epiphany—it was his intense feeling and deep affection for Gabrielle, a tenderness that had escaped him. He'd never before experienced a romantic attachment to someone so deeply. It frightened him, and now he was vulnerable and desired what Gabrielle had experienced her entire life—the love of family and a future of contentment.

"Diego, such courage shouldn't be taken with hostility. No, you showed what every woman would hope to see in a man—integrity, courage, and trust. I love you more now than ever, and as for Paris, I hear Rio is wonderful at this time of year," she said, embracing her future husband.

Gabino and Isubela Santos were overjoyed with the union and introduced their new son-in-law to the other four members of the Tribunal Cinco, who were cordial but mindful that he was a foreigner and would never be a member of their association. The Santos' understood the tribunal's position, but that had no bearing on their ranch or future dealings with the other owners, as Gabrielle was the heir apparent and the future patroness. The matter was a moot point, as the Santos' were the youngest of the five ranch owners, and their legacy would be well into the future.

The festivities continued into the early hours of the morning. Billy and his bride departed the next day for Rio de Janeiro. They stayed at a five-star hotel for eight days. When they ventured outside of their bedroom, they went sightseeing, basked in the sun on the spectacular Copacabana beach, and dined and danced the evening away while gazing at the stars from the balcony of their bedroom.

On the last day of their honeymoon, they shopped at several stores, buying gifts for friends and family. Billy was searching for a pair of jeans when he looked up and did a double-take when he saw a familiar man across the aisle. He lowered his head, and without warning, he grabbed Gabrielle's arm and put his finger to his lips. Both abruptly left the store and rushed back to the hotel.

Diego, what is going on?" Gabrielle demanded.

"I recognized an associate of that hired killer I testified against."

In fact, Billy had seen Detective Mike Kelly, who had been chasing the ex-priest for several years. Was it a coincidence, or had the detective followed the scent and was only miles away from capturing the man who had killed twelve people?

Chapter 13

Amelioration

TWO YEARS HAD PASSED since the incident in Rio. Billy was unnerved and concerned that at any time, the authorities would be at his doorstep. Gabrielle was in her eighth month of pregnancy, and to the delight of the Santos family, she was expecting a girl. It wasn't an easy pregnancy for the thirty-two year old, who was told to remain in bed during her final month.

Marcela Isubela Montes was born on Saturday, June 12, 2004. The birth was without incident, and when Billy held his daughter in his arms for the first time, he began to cry. The tears of joy, however, couldn't wash away his regret. He was transforming, and it was a frightening experience. Could he alter his brain and rewire his checkerboard circuits that compelled him to stamp out those who opposed his self-interests?

Billy's past arrogance created his own self-absorption and depraved indifference toward those who posed a threat to his indulgent sexuality. The forty-three-year-old's misgivings converged into an effort to alter the earlier period of his life. The reincarnation provided by the Santos family was a fresh start for his humanity.

Fifteen months after the birth of their daughter, Gabrielle had a son, whom they named Gabino, after the grandfather, a cherished tradition in the valley. Billy didn't object, as the name meant "God is my strength."

Billy now was firmly entrenched as foreman of the ranch. He pleased his father-in-law, who was overjoyed that Billy had justified the appointment. The men on the ranch grew to respect Billy, the outsider, and he demanded earnest and conscientious activity every day, while leading by example.

In late June 2005, the Santoses left for vacation in Europe, stopping in Portugal, France, and then London. While riding the subway—something Isubela had wanted to experience—a terrorist's bomb exploded.

It would kill fifty-two passengers, including the Santos'.

"Gabino, my love, riding in this subway has been a fantasy of mine since I was a child. I've heard stories of the trains that travel under the streets of London, and I can't believe that I'm here. Thank you, my husband."

"Isubela, the smile on your face is all the thanks I need. You have been the center of my life and I'll always be grateful for your love and devotion."

Suddenly, the detonation was deafening, and the wrenching of metal was ear-piercing.

"Gabino, what is happening?" Isubela cried.

"It's an explosion, Isubela. Stay low, my love."

"I'm frightened, *mi amor.*"

These were the last words that Isubela spoke. The explosion released projectiles and poisonous fumes throughout the twisted wreckage. Gabino reached for his wife, even though a jagged piece of metal was protruding from his chest cavity. His fingers crawled to find Isubela, and the meeting of their hands was forged with his last breath of life.

The news of the tragedy, sent shockwaves throughout the valley. Gabrielle, overwhelmed with sorrow, was now patroness of the Santos ranch. Her parents would never see the September birth of her son. It would take fifteen-days before the bodies of her parents were released.

The funeral and burial ceremony for Isubela and Gabino took place on their ranch; the bodies were laid to rest in the family cemetery. It would be months before Gabrielle would meet with the other four members of the Tribunal Cinco. When they did, a review of their bylaws resulted in emphasizing the alignment of ownership. They revisited their law of foreign ownership and etched out a line of succession in the event of Gabrielle's passing. The ranch would be placed in trust for the children and co-managed by the surviving ranchers. Billy would maintain his position as foreman but comply with the rulings of the tribunal. When one of the children reached the age of twenty-one, control of the ranch would be transferred—that would be Marcela, Gabrielle's daughter, and her son, Gabino, fifteen months afterwards.

Gabrielle's becoming patroness of the ranch was ill-timed. Her second pregnancy, coupled with the passing of her parents, left little room for the daily management of the cattle farm. Although her husband was denied the succession of ownership, he made all the decisions for the ranch. Gabrielle was absorbed with raising the children, although impeded by the death of her parents. She was a doting mother—her remedy for sorrow and depression.

Billy had been transformed. No longer was he the angry, vengeful ex-priest; now, he was a devoted husband and father. His past seemed to have vanished, as though it never existed. Anyone meeting the man of the Santos ranch would have the impression that he was a consummate husband and father, and a savvy businessman. He was a distinguished speaker when in the company of others and was looked upon as someone who should be in the business of politics and cultivate the future of the ranching community. He had ameliorated his persona and was loved by his family, friends, and coworkers. His relationship with Gabrielle grew stronger; he was steadfastly in love with her and fascinated by her seductive path to their relationship and her fastidious approach to her appearance.

Billy felt safe and was content with his role on the ranch. All was going well for the former priest, and the recurring nightmares of those he had killed slowly disappeared.

The Investigation

Still festering were two detectives from Boston who had sworn to capture the murderer and monster who killed the teenage daughter of Detective Nick Stone. They had been working leads since Billy's disappearance, focusing on those countries with no extradition agreement with the United States.

"Mike, we've been chasing Pratt for almost three years, and all we have to show for it is dead end after dead end. Maybe we're taking the wrong approach," Stone said, his weariness clearly showing.

"How's that?" Mike asked.

"What if this guy anticipated our approach and did a flip-flop?"

"Nick, are you suggesting he'd take the chance of fleeing to a country with an extradition agreement with us?"

"Yes, it makes sense. When did you ever work a case that went this cold after a year, and we're at year three?"

"Okay, but the world is a big place, and this guy has shown that he's not afraid to explore it. Where do we start?" asked Kelly.

"Your guess is as good as mine. Pick a continent—Europe, Asia, or South America?"

"Let's do this," Mike suggested. "I'll take Europe; you take South America. We'll ask the law enforcement of each country if they've seen the Interpol description of Pratt and then check with all of their municipalities, asking if any Americans have resided in their districts in the last three years who fit the profile."

The two detectives spoke to their captain of their new approach, and he gave his blessing—with a caveat. "Think of the number of cold cases that never get solved. Your search shouldn't be at the expense of your current workload. You can't allow your emotions to overshadow reality. Sometimes, you just have to let go and move on."

The captain's words hit home with Mike but not with Nick. With Nick, it was personal. His daughter's killer had to pay.

Chapter 14

One Year Later

THE DEATH OF A Tribunal Cinco member became the opportunity for Billy and Gabrielle to expand their holdings. Under the tribunal charter, if a member passed away without heirs, the remaining ranch owners could bid for the property, and the proceeds set aside in accordance to the will of the landowner. There were now four members of the Tribunal Cinco, with Gabrielle the most prominent. The other three ranch owners paid homage to the patroness, but in the state of things, it was Billy from whom they sought leadership when the political environment might result in damaging their interests.

When new legislation was proposed to increase taxes of cattle farms, the tribunal members charged Billy, as their ambassador, to tranquilize the measure. When he succeeded in convincing the taxing authorities of the burden that would be placed on the ranchers if the new measures were enacted, the rate of increase was significantly reduced.

Billy was no longer looked upon as the gringo outsider. He'd gained respect from the current members and was now involved in all tribunal business. Within six months, another tribunal member died, leaving the ranch to his son, as his wife had passed six years earlier. The son wanted no part of the lifestyle he'd endured since a child and sold his interest to the highest bidder, patroness Gabrielle Montes.

The three remaining ranchers met and agreed to reform the bylaws of the tribunal; the most significant change allowed Diego Montes a chair at the council. The gesture paid tribute to the man they previously called an outsider and now granted ownership rights to the ex-priest; the Santos family became owners of the largest ranch in the valley.

That evening's sunset cast a specular prism of colors over the horizon. Billy and Gabrielle were sitting on a loveseat, with her head nestled on his shoulder, their children playing with the family dog.

"Diego, my love, the tribunal bestowed a great honor upon you. You've been accepted as one of us, an honor that hasn't been given to a non-Brazilian since the inception of the tribunal charter. My father and mother would be proud … as I am. We're in a good place, my husband. God has blessed our family, bringing you to me and our beautiful children. But there are things I wish to discuss with you, mi amor, that are extremely important to me."

"What is it, Gabrielle?" Billy asked.

"Now that the charter laws of the tribunal have been changed, it's imperative to have our legal papers modified. If something should happen to me or to both of us, I want the ranch to be yours or the children's. I don't want my family's history and what they created to be blacked out or to fall into the hands of the other members or an outsider. Also, tomorrow, before the ten o'clock mass, the priests are hearing holy confession, and I want us to cleanse our souls."

Gabrielle continued to speak, but Billy wasn't listening. He visualized the confessional when he had been a priest and had tuned into those who fed his sexual appetite or who he considered pathetic for their weaknesses. The faces of his victims reappeared and demanded recognition from the ex-priest. Each killing was a vivid portrayal of his past trespasses. He began to perspire; beads of sweat appeared on his brow.

Concerned for his well-being, Gabrielle asked, "Diego, are you not feeling well?"

"I'm fine, Gabrielle. Your gesture has overwhelmed me. From the very moment we met, you took my breath away, and you do every day of my life, but I don't deserve your respect or that of your parents. The church has deemed my past sins unforgivable. I was excommunicated by the Holy Father himself. I blaspheme every time I step into church or receive holy communion. The host singes my very soul and marks the coming of my eternal damnation." Billy's emotions were unlocked as he exposed his self-condemnation.

"Diego, my love, God has infinite forgiveness, no matter our past sins."

"That may be, but how does one forgive one's own dishonor?"

Gabrielle turned to her husband and embraced the man she loved without judgment and without interrogating him for hidden truths. She respected his wishes and did not press him on his fragile issues. She did, however, arrange to meet with her attorney and make the changes to her will, coordinating Diego's as well.

Detectives at Work

Several thousand miles away in a Boston precinct, two detectives were narrowing the number of countries that Billy could have chosen for his Houdini-like escape.

Stone seemed dejected over the search. "Mike, I don't see the priest leaving for Europe, Asia, or Africa. I've checked for all plausible ports of entry, municipalities, villages, and hamlets. It's like looking for a needle in a gigantic haystack."

"I may have found that needle, Nick," said Kelly, tantalizing his partner. "There are five men with similar descriptions who fit the profile of our priest. Believe it or not, two are practicing clerics in Argentina, another is in Paraguay, one is in Peru, and one is in Brazil." Kelly was unaware of his close proximity to the killer when he'd vacationed in Rio de Janeiro, and the murderer was on his honeymoon.

"Where do we go from here?" Nick asked.

"Let's talk to the captain and see what leeway we have."

The chief had previously told the two detectives to back off, and now his response to their request to pursue leads in the four countries was flatly denied.

"It's officially a cold case, and I insist you treat it as an unresolved investigation. There are other cases that have priority, and the inspector is breathing down my neck for better numbers, so both of you get your asses in gear and forget Pratt. Are we clear?"

The captain's stinging ultimatum resonated with both men.

"Well, that's your answer, Nick," Mike said later. "Look, he didn't say anything about pursuing this on our own time. If it's gnawing in your gut, why don't we follow the leads on our own? If we do, though, it's got to be covert."

Kelly had his own reasons for wanting to capture the ex-priest but none was more compelling than his partner's desire to capture the man who had murdered his daughter. Both men had been in law enforcement for a number of years and had been approached by relatives and friends who wanted justice or revenge on criminals who had harmed their loved ones. The emotion was no different for the men in blue, though they were held to a higher standard when serving the public.

The two detectives divided the leads. Nick followed the suspects in Peru and Argentina, while Mike followed the evidence in Paraguay and Brazil. They would work independently, with their vacation time spent in designated countries. Both realized their approach would require time and money, but each had a score to settle with the killer.

Nick had remained single after his divorce, so his time was his own. Mike on the other hand was now married; he'd taken the first step to a fresh beginning. His new wife was an assistant district attorney with deep family ties to the police department. Their vacation time spent in pursuing a killer would have been a difficult challenge to the best of relationships. Still, the murder of his former partner, Maggie Burns, had to be avenged. But at what cost?

Bliss in Brazil

Gabrielle was in the second trimester of her third pregnancy. The pregnancy hadn't been planned, and there was deep concern for her health, as the previous pregnancies had taken a toll. Billy coordinated the daily management of the ranch, and he delegated responsibilities. The ranch was highly profitable, which created the green-eyed monster in the two remaining tribunal members; they were overwhelmed with envy. Billy offered to review their business practices, and in each case, significant waste of resources was draining their profitability.

In the beginning, the two ranch owners had reservations about accepting Billy's suggestions—they didn't want to concede their own weaknesses—but in the end, Billy's ideas had an impact on their bottom line, and they were once again competitive. The indebted ranchers proposed a consortium, led by Billy. He would lay the course of operations for the three remaining ranches and would have inviolable authority.

By the time his second son was born, Billy's influence in the valley had reached epic proportions—inconceivable for a so-called foreigner. His name became known in the far corners of the Brazilian ranching community. His ideas were transforming, and he was sought out by several of his contemporaries in the industry as his popularity gained momentum.

Another year had passed, and the world of Diego Montes couldn't have been brighter. He had a devoted wife, three healthy children, a booming business, and the respect of his community. How did a man who was a killer of twelve reshuffle his life with this enormous modification? Could an unexpected event change the former priest? He would be tested. His double life of metamorphic conversion might prove to be his final betrayal.

Chapter 15

Reckless Indiscretion

CALLS FOR BILLY TO run for political office were gaining strength in the districts represented by the powerful ranchers of Sao Paulo, who all profited from his guidance. His wife encouraged his foray into politics, as she'd noticed her husband was fatigued by the daily responsibilities of the ranch, and she thought a new challenge might energize the father of three.

Diego Santos Montes Jr., Gabrielle and Billy's second son, came into the world without complications. He would be their final child.

"My husband, it's a great honor that the party wishes to bestow upon you—running for governor of Sao Paulo. How wonderful it would be for the valley and our family," Gabrielle said.

Billy smiled at his wife and contemplated the significance of political life for him and the family. It would be a different world from managing the ranch. He'd be away from the family for several days at a time, and that was a point of contention, but Gabrielle assured her husband the sacrifice would bring self-satisfaction and honor to the family. He ignored that he was a fugitive, a wanted man who had murdered people and that a high-profile arena could eventually result in his downfall. The scent of center stage was no different than when he was preaching before his parishioners, when all eyes were upon him, and every word he spoke was taken as the gospel truth.

But there were some who wanted more.

"What do we know about this gringo? How can a man come to our country and gain status in a few years? Every man has stain under his fingernails. I want to know where he came from and the dirt he carried to our country," said the leader of the opposition party, whose candidate was born in the district.

Days later, Billy met with his endorsers—the wealthy ranchers beyond the valley who were ready to declare their champion candidate. He was assigned a political adviser to guide him through the coming scrutiny from the opposition. The meeting had shaken Billy; he was naive in the ways of politics and hadn't anticipated the required information about his family history. He told the coordinator he wasn't feeling well and asked to reschedule the meeting; the political adviser was taken aback.

As Billy left for home, he was having second thoughts about running for governor. Perhaps he had been reckless in accepting the endorsement. He was in a panic and raced to the library, trying to fabricate a history that was impossible to trace. How could he disguise the chronicle of a murderous ex-priest who had avoided the authorities for years? He had to recreate a persona—one that would pass the scrutiny of the opposition while maintaining his camouflage under the name Diego Montes.

A week passed, and Billy's political coordinator pressed him for a meeting. He prepared for questions he considered obligatory and that would be examined by the opposition. He said he was raised in Thousand Oaks, Texas, by his father, Ramon, and mother, Cynthia, both of whom had been killed in a car accident when he was thirty years old. He had earned a bachelor's degree in psychology from the University of Texas and had worked at various jobs until leaving the United States and settling in Brazil. His story was pieced together, yet it could be verified by anyone who investigated his background. He had googled every known family with the last name of Montes that lived in the United States and who were at least seventy-years old.

Ramon and Cynthia Montes had a son named Diego who had disappeared when he was thirty years old. The case was unsolved and was buried in the cold-case files of the Thousand Oaks Police Department. It was the perfect cover and obscured Billy's real identity. He secured the social security number of the missing son when he asked the police if the case of Diego Montes was still active. A police sergeant inadvertently volunteered the information when distinguishing the father from the son.

The ex-priest was back to his old ways of lying, cheating, and doing what was necessary to achieve his end. He took a moment to think about abandoning the charade and what it would mean to his family if he was discovered. He had orchestrated a house of cards, a bubble that could implode from any unforeseen crisis. But he dismissed the thought of surrender. His reckless indiscretion was fueled by the euphoria of once again leading a flock.

He explained the necessity of the ruse to Gabrielle. "If information of my excommunication were revealed in our Catholic-dominated community, I'll easily be defeated."

His wife was complicit by her acceptance.

Billy's political backers were satisfied the opposition would find nothing to prevent their candidate from winning the election, and they were right. Diego Montes became the newly elected governor of the largest city in Brazil. When the results were officially announced, the celebration in the valley of their favorite son lasted through the night.

"My husband, words cannot express how proud I feel at this moment. Look, Diego, a shooting star over the horizon. It's a sign from above, celebrating your destiny." Gabrielle placed her hand to his heart. It was a tender moment for both; they embraced and looked at the crescent moon together.

The next morning, Billy's chauffeur arrived at the ranch at 7:30 A.M, as he had directed. His official office was now in Sao Paulo, a fifty-five minute drive from the ranch. When he and Gabrielle reached their destination, they were greeted by several well-wishers and his transitional staff. Within the hour, Diego was officially sworn in as the new governor, with his wife by his side.

Two years into his four year administration, Diego Montes faced his first political crisis. Those responsible for his election were seeking reimbursement from the governor. The assembly of influential ranchers demanded two vital changes in the law. The previous administration's tax increase on cattle ranches, although weakened by the man who now held office, was squeezing their profits due to the precipitous fall in cattle prices. Competition from Argentinian beef was flooding the market, and the ranchers wanted a district tariff imposed on all cattle entering Sao Paulo, excluding Brazilian beef.

Diego was sympathetic to the ranchers' dilemma, but he accurately stated it wasn't within the power of his office to institute a tariff on imports to Sao Paulo; only the president of Brazil could impose the special tax. His conclusion was not taken well by his supporters, who now doubted his loyalty.

The resolution came from an unlikely source after a respite of intimacy. "My husband, you seem oceans away from me. What's going on in this cabesa?" Gabrielle asked, pointing to her husband's head.

The governor explained the crisis he was facing from his supporters. "My hands are tied by Brazilian law," he said.

His wife propped herself up on a pillow to support her back. The sheet covering her body slipped below, exposing her breast, and Billy seized the moment.

"Stop, Diego," Gabrielle said, playfully pushing his head from her bosom. "My husband, I think I have a solution for your ranchers. This is simply a supply-and-demand issue. If truckers delivering beef were required to be union members, the cost of delivery would increase, and if our ranchers temporarily cut back production, prices on beef would increase."

He stared at his wife and then smiled, for she had stumbled upon the perfect quick-fix to his problem.

The next day, Billy gathered the displeased ranchers and informed them of his solution to their concerns. All but one supported his proposal; the lone dissenter was concerned that cutting back on production would have an immediate impact on his finances. The ranchers agreed that the governor's actions would initially have a negative impact, but it would be short-lived and would be compensated by pooling their resources to help bolster those in need.

Billy had successfully managed his first political crisis as governor, but what he and his wife were about to endure would have no resolution.

Chapter 16
The Stain of Past Sins

THE NEW LAW REQUIRING truckers to be members of the union had a dramatic impact on non-union drivers. Becoming a member wasn't the simple task of filling out a form. Several truckers were out of work and they blamed the governor for their misery.

Billy's daily routine was predictable and carefully monitored. On this day, his family accompanied him to his Sao Paulo office, as they had planned a midday luncheon. Forty-five minutes into their journey, the rear window of the chauffeured car was shattered, forcing the vehicle off the road. Gabrielle screamed in horror. Her daughter lay helplessly in her arms, bleeding from a gunshot wound to her head. She was air-transported to the hospital, but it was in vain. Marcela was pronounced dead on arrival. Their daughter's assassination struck a blow to their hearts; both Billy and Gabrielle were inconsolable.

The massive hunt for the killer produced immediate results. The bad-tempered driver was shot to death in front of his family, as ordered by the governor. Gabrielle demanded that her husband exact the same justice for their daughter's killer that he had levied on her. Gabrielle's eye-for-an-eye mind-set was Billy's first glimpse of her dark side.

Marcela's death was only the beginning of the problems for the Montes family. Three weeks after burying Marcela, their son Gabino was stung by a swarm of wasps while playing outside his home. The insects were the most dangerous and aggressive species in Brazil, and Gabino fell into anaphylactic shock.

He was placed into a medically induced coma, and the doctors were unsure if he would survive or, when the pentobarbital was no longer essential, and if his bodily functions would ever return to normal.

The successive calamities changed the relationship between Billy and Gabrielle, as she suspected that her husband's past deeds were responsible for her children's misfortune. She begged him to confess his sins, before God, in his wrath, exacted further punishment upon the family.

Billy agreed to her demand but only to appease his agitated wife. He had no intention of confessing to the murders of twelve people.

When Gabrielle and Billy lost their son to an existence of confined darkness, they slowly drifted apart. Her entire being was now committed to tending to her son, who was confined to a wheelchair and incontinent. There were few exchanges between the struggling parents and that extended to their intimacy, something they no longer shared. Gabrielle had completely closed down and was a ghost within her own home.

Four months had passed since Billy's son had been stricken, and his loneliness was wearing thin. He no longer went home after performing his duties as governor. They were several women whose claws dug deep and submitted to the aphrodisiac of power. Billy maintained a suite in one of Sao Paulo's five-star hotels and returned to his days of debauchery. There was no discreetness about his after-hours activities. He was to run for reelection within the next fifteen months, and his supporters were concerned that the state of political affairs were fading in the winds of time.

Billy's closest adviser, Miguel Rocha, warned his governor that the opposition party could be planning to use his recent marital troubles as political fodder.

But there was another storm brewing. Gabrielle had heard of her husband's infidelities and didn't intend to be misled or made a fool.

It was the weekend and one of the few the governor spent at the hacienda. After dinner, Gabrielle opened a manila envelope in front of Billy and scattered several photos of his being in a compromising embrace with a woman.

Billy was speechless and taken aback. The woman he once said could take his breath away was now opposing his way of life.

"What do you want me to say, Gabrielle? That the photos are a lie? Because they're not, and you want to know why? Since Marcela's death and Gabino's affliction, you've been a scourge in our house, blaming me for their tragedies. Your meltdown of the woman I once knew has torn the heart from my chest."

He continued to deflect blame for his behavior, and when he finally was silent, it was Gabrielle's turn.

"You know when I became your so-called scourge? It was the day Father Lopez told me that you never confessed your sins. God hasn't forgiven you because you haven't asked him for forgiveness. If the stain of past sins is so reprehensible that absolution is unimaginable in your eyes, how do you expect our house to be forgiven and safe from the pestilence raining down from the heavens? I've advised my attorneys to remove you as the benefactor of the hacienda and from all other assets of my estate. You're no longer welcome in this house. You can expect to be served with divorce papers on Monday. The Tribunal Cinco has been notified and your participation has been revoked."

Their once-unconquerable bond was shattered by her husband's betrayal.

Billy's deceit and lechery was outmaneuvered by Gabrielle. She had stamped him out of her life, and she was no longer an ally but a threat, which didn't bode well for those who stood in his way. He gathered some of his belongings and told his wife he'd send for the rest. He kissed his sons, Gabino and Diego. When he attempted to show the same affection to his wife, she shunned the gesture and turned away from the man she had ripped from her life.

"Are you sure you want to do this, Gabrielle?" he asked, staring at his wife from the doorway of their home.

Gabrielle closed the door in response.

The governor left for his apartment in Sao Paulo, and after he arrived, the concierge personally delivered an envelope to him. Billy placed his briefcase on the foyer table and walked to the kitchen. He removed a kitchen knife from its holder and slit the envelope open. After reading the message, he crumpled the paper and lashed out at the items on the table—glasses shattered on impact, and a plate of fruit was dispersed across the room.

There it was—the crumpled message from the father of the daughter he had killed. The note wasn't detailed; it simply read, "I believe you have a murderer in your town."

Billy called Miguel Rocha to his suite, and within a half hour, the political adviser was at his door.

"Miguel, you're my most trusted adviser, and what we're about to discuss must remain in this room. Can I depend on your allegiance?"

"Yes, Governor, on the soul of my family."

"Good, good, Miguel," said Billy, tapping the adviser on his shoulder. He informed him of his impending divorce and that he was leaving Sao Paulo for two weeks. "I'm overcome with grief and need to clear my mind in preparation for the coming challenges before the election. Tell anyone who asks about my whereabouts that I'm on a working holiday. If you're asked whether my family accompanied him, say that Mrs. Montes stayed at home to be with the children."

"Where will you go, my Governor?" Rocha, asked.

"Miguel, it's best that you don't know, my friend. What you don't know you can't reveal. You're to be my intermediary on all issues, and I will instruct my secretary to have inquiries or messages directed to you. Take careful details of all requests, who made them, and where they can be reached. Expect my call every day at four o'clock for a report. My trusted friend, can you do this for me?"

The political adviser assured the governor that his dictum would be followed.

It was what the governor didn't reveal that was the driving force of his leaving Sao Paulo that Sunday evening.

On Monday, Billy called Miguel at four o'clock, asking for a summary of the day's events.

"A process server came to your office, asking where you were," Miguel said. "You had the usual requests for an audience, but none was essential. I did find one visitor to the office a bit mystifying. A New York City detective named Nick Stone, requested an interview."

Stone wasn't supposed to be in Brazil; he was to investigate Peru and Argentina. But he switched with Kelly, as he wanted to see Brazil, leaving Argentina to his partner.

Miguel told Billy where the police detective was staying and gave Billy his cell phone number. That evening, Billy called the detective from a disposable phone, explaining that he was on a working vacation in Peru, the country where Stone had previously spent three days searching for his daughter's killer.

"Governor, do you recognize the description of the man I'm hunting?" Stone asked.

"It sounds like a man who was working as my foreman on the ranch, Galtero Gomes," Billy said. Gomes was the person who tried to kill Billy because he was jealous of Gabrielle's fondness for the outsider.

"Where can I find the man?" Stone asked.

"Gomes never showed up for work one day," Billy said, "and no one has heard from him since then. Perhaps he knew the police were getting close to discovering his whereabouts and he decided to leave the country."

Unbeknownst to the detective, Billy had a plan to eliminate the threat of him being exposed. He checked into the same motel where Stone was staying, using a false name and a disguise so deceptive that his own staff wouldn't have recognized his identity.

The switch had been flipped, and the reformed father of three was now the person who eliminated those who threatened his course of actions. He knew if Stone was murdered, it would draw the attention of the Boston Police to Sao Paulo. It had to appear an unfortunate accident. It was not unusual for poisonous snakes and spiders to lurk in urban areas. In fact, snakebites were known to happen in urban areas, and Sao Paulo was a hotbed for rattlesnakes.

Just as an addict can find a fix anywhere in the world, so can a criminal find someone for hire to do a felonious task for the right price. Billy paid the asking price.

It was three o'clock in the morning when the two outlaws slid a credit card along the door lock. The detective was sound asleep. To ensure a state of deep sleep, a towel laced with chloroform was placed on his face, incapacitating him. The criminals planned to restrain their victim when administering the toxin, but the sleeping pill Stone had taken that night cleared the way for their treachery. Two rattlesnakes were placed in the bed of the unsuspecting cop, and then both men left the room.

The next morning, the cleaning lady found Stone dead, with the snakes still in his bed.

After verifying the successful transaction, Billy left the motel for Paraguay, arranging to meet with the governor of Alto. He told his counterpart he wished to exchange ideas to see how he could improve his people's standard of living. The planned meeting was held in Asuncion.

Billy's final day in Paraguay was spent at the pool of the five-star hotel. He was sipping on a *mosto*, a sugarcane juice, spiked with vodka, while gawking at women in their skimpy bikinis and envisioning two of them fulfilling his most erotic desires.

But there were more important issues to resolve. He had been stripped of his family, and the powerful ranchers who supported his election would seek a more viable candidate; Gabrielle would see to that. Her pedigree meant a great deal, and divorcing her husband would be fodder for the opposition. Billy had limited choices. He could try to gather the support he needed for reelection or take the more realistic approach. He always survived when his instincts told him to flee the danger surrounding his freedom. He also considered the possibility that the Boston police would investigate Stone's death, and he reminded himself of the extradition treaty between Brazil and the United States. He was older now, and to create a new existence was unappealing, but the alternative was confinement for the rest of his life—or execution.

The news of Nick Stone's death came as a shock to Mike Kelly and those who worked with the fallen detective. It was one thing to be killed in the line of duty, fighting off a felon, but to succumb to a snakebite was unbefitting. It was so unbelievable, but the detective's death was perceived as his being in the wrong place at the wrong time—a bad break and miserable luck.

But Mike wasn't convinced and decided to conduct his own investigation. His new captain encouraged the scrutiny.

Chapter 17
The Decision

THE FLIGHT TO CARACAS, Venezuela, covered about twenty-seven hundred miles. Billy was desperate to return to the country where he was a wanted man, and responsible for two murders. He gambled that the killing of his live-in girlfriend and her brother was an inactive investigation in Coro, miles from Caracas. He relied upon the change in his appearance to deflect recognition of those who could possibly identify him. He now sported a full beard and ponytail. The country was safe from the Boston police. There still was no extradition treaty with the United States and relations had been strained for several years.

Billy decided to completely uncouple from his life in Brazil. It was a callous approach, as he gave his two surviving children no consideration in his decision. He was now in a survival mode. The switch had been flipped, and sympathy was ripped from his thought process. He rented a modest apartment and started the hunt for employment. Choices were limited to the cattle or oil industry for Victor Dias, his new alias. He chose the one having access to leaving the country at a moment's notice. His experience was in great demand and he was immediately hired by a domestic oil company in Venezuela.

The first week of work was a testament to Billy's spending most of his day in an office for three years. His body ached, and his hands were blistered; he placed them in saltwater each evening before retiring. The month was an audition for Billy's employers, and they were impressed by his insight and work acumen. He stayed mostly to himself; his fellow workers were unaware he was an American.

His complexion had darkened over the years, and he could have easily been considered a native South American. It wouldn't be long before he sought female companionship. The local bars and brothels were filled with women seeking relief from the economic and political chaos within their country.

One evening, Billy stopped at a local club that was playing live music. He ordered a beer, and within five minutes, he was approached by three ladies of the night, each auditioning their wares. When he showed little interest, so did the solicitation. After ordering a steak sandwich and a second beer, a woman sat in the chair next to him. She was different from the others who'd approached him. She looked more like a professional businesswoman than a lady of the night. She didn't speak or even look in his direction, which aroused his curiosity. When she ordered a glass of champagne, it paved the way for him to be friendly.

"May I have the pleasure of buying the drink you ordered?" Billy asked the elegant and polished woman, who smiled and nodded her acceptance.

"My name is Victor, and I would like very much to know yours," he said kindly and with a sincere smile.

"Rachael. Rachael Torres," responded the woman, returning the tenderness.

The two engaged in conversation for the next forty-five minutes and then departed for his apartment. When they entered the three-room flat, Billy poured drinks, and after a brief period, he attempted to kiss the nape of Rachael's neck. She placed her hand to his face and gently nudged his head away.

She stood from the couch and said, "Shall we first address the financial matter?"

Billy was confused, thinking that his charm had prompted her to return to his apartment. After overcoming his consternation, he wanted to know the charge. She responded in Venezuelan currency, the bolivar. She saw him hesitate but didn't know he was American and trying to convert the value of the bolivar to the dollar. When he realized she was demanding seventy-five dollars for her services, he placed the money on a nearby table. Rachael retrieved the bolivars and put them in her purse.

The nearly two hours he spent with the woman were the most enjoyable since fleeing Brazil. She was extremely attractive, a lighter brown than most women of her country. She was five-six and a modest one-hundred-thirty pounds. Her eyes were brown, as was her shoulder-length hair.

Billy asked why she resorted to prostitution.

"I had a job with an American company that closed its operation," Rachael explained. "I couldn't find work. Most women in Caracas are unemployed due to government corruption and are forced into prostitution in order to survive."

He really liked Rachael; she was polished and sincere. Billy asked her to have dinner with him the following evening, and Rachael accepted. She didn't request payment for her friendship, which was appreciated by the fugitive from the United States and taken as a sign that she wanted to enhance the relationship.

The Boston Chase

The media outlets headlined the mysterious disappearance of their governor. The speculations were diverse, one suggesting that Governor Montes had committed suicide because of his impending divorce, and another speculating that he'd been kidnapped by those who opposed the reduction of tax imposed upon the ranchers.

The story was picked up by the international media and made curious reading for Mike Kelly. The death of his partner and the disappearance of Diego Montes, created an interesting mental picture in the detective's mind. He sipped on his coffee, and his eyes were fixated on the window as he tried to organize his thoughts. He curled his lip and placed his coffee on the desk. Then he scowled, frustrated with his disorganized and fragmented conclusions. Mike slapped his desk out of frustration and scuttled to the bathroom. He relieved himself and washed his hands, splashing cold water to his face. He returned to his desk, refilled his coffee cup, and continued his deliberation.

All of a sudden, the picture took shape. Could the ex-priest and the governor be one and the same person? Could it be that Nick Stone's death wasn't an accident but murder? He shook his head in disbelief, scoffing at the idea that the killer priest could become the governor of a city in South America. Then, he remembered what the priest had said to him during an interrogation in regard to the death of Monsignor Gaston. *"Like the chameleon who adapts to his enemies, what seems obvious can confuse and astonish the best of those who pursue."*

The priest attempted to deflect suspicion that the death of three priests wasn't an accident but premeditated murder.

Mike briefed his commander of his insight on Nick Stone's death and the disappearance of the governor in Sao Paulo.

"Kelly, are you kidding me? You believe that a guy who killed twelve people became the governor of the largest city in Brazil? Mike, I've given you a lot of latitude, but Jesus, if I told the deputy chief your theory, he'd commit us both to the psych ward."

Mike made his case for pursuing the investigation by going to San Paulo. "Captain, I know it seems far-fetched, but this guy is no ordinary felon. He's educated, street-smart, and a shrewd son of a bitch. You yourself have preached that a cop's instinct is his 'guts positioning system.' Maybe my hunch doesn't wash, but what if I'm right? We catch the bastard, and we make our bones, while bringing peace to the family of his victims, including one of our own."

The chief turned away from his detective and gazed out the window of his office, trying to determine what his posture should be on this request. He turned, facing Kelly, and then gave him the go-ahead to follow his hunch.

When Mike arrived home, he addressed the meeting with his captain and informed his wife that he would be leaving for Brazil in the morning.

"Mike, when are you going to let go of this? It's consumed you for years and affected our marriage."

"Angie, you came from a family of cops. You, of all people, should know there's always one case that defines the career of a detective. I can't let it go and just fade away from it. I have to nail this bastard, or it'll stalk me forever."

"I don't know if I can handle this, Mike. We've both been through failed relationships. Can't you demonstrate the same passion in our marriage as you have with your obsession to catch this man? It may destroy what's left of what we have. Let it go, Mike, for our sake."

"It's been difficult for you—I know it has—but this is who I am, Angie. I can't let go. I won't let this guy define my career as a failure. I leave in the morning, and when I get back, I promise to make it up to you. Please, Angie, I'm begging you to be here for me."

The Chase in Brazil

Kelly left for Brazil the next day, arriving in Sao Paulo by late afternoon. He requested an audience with Miguel Rocha, the governor's political adviser. The meeting was arranged for the following morning.

"Mr. Rocha, thank you for taking time from your busy schedule to see me. The Boston Police Department has been tracking a prolific killer for several years, and we believe he may be or has been in your country, perhaps here in Sao Paulo."

"Detective Kelly, what makes you think your man is in our city?"

"My partner, Detective Nick Stone, was found by your police in his motel room, killed by two rattlesnakes."

"What does that have to do with the man you're looking for? Unfortunately, we have several deaths from poisonous snakes every year," Rocha said.

"I'm working on a premise that there's little coincidence when dealing with hardened criminals. Your governor disappeared at the same time of Detective Stone's death. I believe that the man that I'm pursuing … is your missing governor."

"That seems preposterous, Detective Kelly. Governor Montes has been an upstanding citizen and represents a prominent Sao Paulo family." Rocha stood, indicating the meeting was at an end.

"Hold on, Mr. Rocha; stay with me for a moment. Was Mr. Montes born in Sao Paulo or anywhere else in Brazil? From what I read about the man, he appeared out of nowhere and within a few years became the leader of your city. Why has he suddenly disappeared at the same time my partner was found dead?"

"Mr. Kelly, the governor left our city because of personal family problems; he needed to clear his head."

"Sir, I understand he's been away for a substantial period and has been declared missing. A coincidence? I don't think so, Mr. Rocha, and there's one way to prove me wrong or clarify the history of Sao Paulo. Do you have a photo or portrait of the governor?"

The political adviser was torn between being a loyal soldier or being a hostile co-conspirator in obstructing justice. He hadn't heard from the governor for several weeks, and at times, he felt abandoned. He had to make a choice, as he feared the Boston detective would seek answers elsewhere. He opened a drawer and retrieved an envelope. When he sat at his desk, he looked at the detective and hesitated over whether he should continue. Finally, he placed a photo of the governor on his desk, facing Kelly.

When the detective saw the image, the expression on his face was one of astonishment. He opened his briefcase and placed a picture of his killer fugitive, side-by-side with the governor's photo.

Rocha raised his head, bewildered and taken aback by the resemblance.

Kelly settled back in his chair, his shoulders slumped, trying to collect his thoughts. He had finally caught up with his accursed nemesis and the killer of thirteen souls—he was now convinced that Billy was responsible for his partner's death. He spent the next four hours gathering the history of Diego Montes, from the time of his partnership with Alec D'Souza to his infiltration into the Santos family, his marriage, and his rise as governor.

Kelly was astounded by the transformation of the ex-priest from ruthless killer to a father of three and a pillar of Sao Paulo society. He alerted his captain of his discovery and explained the fugitive was on the run and that he'd had substantial time to make a getaway.

"Mike, are you serious? That son of a bitch was a family man and governor of a city? I've been a cop for almost thirty-five years, and I must admit, this takes the cake. What a pair of cojones on this guy—unbelievable. Okay, Mike, how much time do you need to wrap this up?"

"Captain, I'm done here and will be leaving tomorrow. I suggest you notify Interpol and all South American authorities of the fugitive's flight from Sao Paulo. Maybe we'll get lucky before I die on this job."

"Good work, Mike. Your instincts were right. The bosses are going to flip when they hear this story; it's one for the books. Have a safe flight, my friend."

Later, Mike sat in the hotel lounge, sipping on his drink. He had come to realize that Billy could be anywhere, and he was back to square one in his pursuit of the killer. The case had unusual dynamics, and although he would take a shoot-to-kill stance, if need be, he had a certain amount of reverence toward the ex-priest. He considered Billy an unsavory and wicked person, but inwardly, he admired his adroitness and versatility. He questioned how a person could be malevolent and shadowy for a number of years and then boldly modify his universe. The more he deliberated on this idea, the more his interpretation of the man was paralyzing. Was it pure arrogance or a perpetuation of immorality— an event in his life being the catalyst that ignited a killer? His consumption of alcohol was blurring his clarity. He was about to retire for the evening when he was approached by Miguel Rocha.

"May I join you, Detective Kelly?"

"Pull up a chair, my friend. We have a common subject to commiserate upon."

Rocha took a seat and ordered a drink. "I'm still traumatized by the turn of events, Detective Kelly. Frankly, I feel simpleminded and shortsighted. I'm supposed to verify the credentials of my party's candidate and handle the vetting of his background. I failed in my responsibility."

"Miguel, I've been chasing this imposter for years. When he was killing people in my town, we had several opportunities to capture this bag of garbage, but we didn't. So, my friend, drink up and allow the stupor of alcohol to dull your feeling of complicity." The detective snickered, attempting to shore up the dejected adviser.

"That's very kind of you, Detective, but tomorrow you leave our country, and I'll still be here to face the music for my failures—a disgraced political adviser with no future."

Before Kelly could respond to Rocha, the despondent man retrieved a pistol from his jacket, placed it under his chin, and pulled the trigger. Brain matter and blood flew in the detective's direction, and his face was splattered with it. After the initial shock, Mike put his hand to his chin and wept. His tough exterior had been cracked, and Rocha's suicide eclipsed any residue of consideration for the killer he was pursuing. He left the next morning for Boston.

The people of Sao Paulo were astonished when the story broke about their governor. Fingers were pointed, each blaming another for the travesty.

Gabrielle Santos was enlightened by her former husband's reluctance to confess his transgressions. She was convinced her children's misfortune was punishment for the sins of their father. She later would be diagnosed with stage-four breast cancer and succumb to her affliction within months. She would die in misery, her estate left in trust for her two surviving children.

Chapter 18

Another Challenge

THE ELUSIVE KILLER HAD settled in a new life in Caracas as Victor Dias and was working for a Venezuelan oil company. Rachael had moved in with him and was three months pregnant with their first child. She was fifteen years younger than Billy, who was now fifty. They lived in a modest two-bedroom apartment, fifteen minutes from his job. When a position opened at his company for an administrative assistant, Rachael applied and was hired. She didn't indicate that she was pregnant at the time and her body didn't betray her. She hoped her performance would warrant her continuation in the position. It was convenient working for the same company with her lover, and she made it clear they were a couple by using the surname, Dias.

In the brief time working for the domestic oil company, Victor Dias attracted the attention of Moises Husan, his overseer. Men with Billy's experience were a commodity in a country riddled with political uncertainty and rampant bribery. But his boss wasn't a choirboy, Rachael's hiring costing two weeks salary demanded by Husan, a gruff individual who showered every third day to conserve water because of its high price.

One of Husan's workers whispered of his past experience with the new administrative assistant. Husan was grateful for the information.

He lived near Billy and his lady friend and had crossed paths with Rachael in the local market prior to her hiring. He was fixated on the Brazilian beauty.

The move to Caracas was uncertain and stressful for Billy. He continually was looking over his shoulder as a hunted fugitive. Leaving Sao Paulo was a shattering experience for the ex-priest, as it abruptly transformed him from a man of respect to a double-dealing and treacherous criminal. He'd been well fixed in his position as governor, and from the human side of the killer… in love with a woman he entrusted a part of him that never existed, the pure intoxication of loving another.

Another challenge would be forthcoming for the outlaw. Two months after Rachael was hired and now five months pregnant, Husan approached Billy and handed him a sheet of paper—a wanted poster issued by Interpol.

Billy was aware that his real identity would one day come back to haunt him, but he hadn't expected it this soon. He couldn't deny who he was, so he asked Husan what he wanted to maintain the secrecy of his newfound knowledge. The request would seal the man's fate, as he demanded intimacy with Rachael and twenty-five percent of Billy's weekly income. Billy agreed to the second request but denied the first as he stared down the unshaven and overweight extortionist.

"My information, Mr. Dias—or whoever you are—is that your woman was an available prostitute, so my request shouldn't be unfamiliar to her."

"Be careful what you wish for, Moises. If you read that poster, you know that I'm not a man to be trifled with," Billy warned him.

Husan acquiesced but had other plans for the fugitive, which included collecting more than his original demand. He was playing chess with a master criminal and was out of his element, but Billy was in a double bind. Husan had cut the reward money off the wanted poster before showing it to Billy and would never be satisfied with a measly twenty-five percent of Billy's income when he could collect a reward of a half million dollars.

Once Billy dealt with the extortionist, he realized his time in Venezuela was limited, but escaping with a pregnant girlfriend was a dilemma. He was addressing a situation with Rachael, as he had with Gabrielle in Sao Paulo.

Billy was at a crossroads and had to make some quick and hard decisions. The slayer was fatigued and mentally depleted; he desired an extended period of calmness and security, but it wasn't in the cards. He considered discussing the current dilemma with Rachael, then offer her a choice of leaving Venezuela with him, or repeat his instincts of survival, killing her and leave the country.

Back in Boston

"Good morning, Captain." Mike Kelly greeted his commander for the first time since his return from Sao Paulo. The ranking officer confirmed that he'd notified Interpol and had forwarded wanted posters to all South American police authorities. They had hoped the significant reward money would lead to the capture of the fugitive ex-priest, but they were unaware that while they were discussing the case, a wanted poster was given to the supervisor of a Venezuelan oil company, who would become the fourteenth victim of the fugitive.

Kelly was in his late fifties and reaching a fatigue level that tested his endurance as an effective detective. His workload was significant, as were the workloads of the other detectives in the squad. The criminal ranks seemingly never ended. He wasn't in particularly good physical condition, and country-jumping to catch the man who had defined his career was taking its toll. He didn't want his life history to be defined by his failure to capture his nemesis.

Mike needed to reenergize. He asked his captain for two weeks of downtime. He was an avid fisherman and decided to vacation with his wife in Rhode Island, hoping to rekindle the spark that once commanded their union. She agreed to stay at a bed-and-breakfast inn; it was quaint but not the Hilton. She had hoped the downtime from the job and his love of fishing would free him from the shackles of the hunt for the killer priest.

The sport took them to Port Judith, where he rented a boat daily and enjoyed the bounty of Block Island and the surrounding area, while his wife inspected the generous shopping malls in the bustling town.

At the end of the day and after a few drinks, Mike would fall into semi-consciousness, and his nightmares would begin. Kelly envisioned a showdown with the killer of his two partners; each time he was bludgeoned to death by the ex-priest, who snickered with each blow. His nightmares were persistent to the point of surrender; his howling screams frightened his wife, who demanded that he seek help. They abandoned the last two days of their planned stay and returned to Boston. Instead of the trip having mended their marriage, the opposite occurred.

Kelly reclaimed his motivation in bringing the ex-priest to justice, but it was the final straw for his beleaguered wife. She recognized that she had lost the man who had swept her off her feet when they first met in a Boston courtroom.

"I'm done, Mike. This isn't what I signed up for. You're not the same man I met three years ago, and I see that it's impossible to recapture what we had. You stay in the apartment, Mike. I'll be moving out by the end of the week."

The detective had struck out for the third time.

Four Years Earlier

"Hello, Detective Kelly. I'm Assistant District Attorney Angie Callahan. I'd like to review your testimony before I call you as a witness for the state."

So started the professional relationship between the two before they became romantically involved. The case was of particular importance to the young prosecutor, and Kelly's testimony was key to her case. The criminal was convicted, and Callahan thanked the detective for giving the precise details of the investigation. Three weeks later, sheer coincidence brought the two together in the same courtroom, although the circumstances were entirely different. The detective's testimony was crucial for the defense in exonerating a man who was accused of manslaughter. It was unusual for a prosecutor to dispute the testimony of a Boston detective. Callahan questioned the cop and disagreed with pivotal testimony.

"How can you be so sure, Detective Kelly?" She had made the critical mistake of asking a question to which she didn't know the answer, and it would cost her the case.

"Because, Ms. Callahan, I happen to be in the bar when the accused was accosted by the deceased. He was minding his own business when the fight broke out. He wasn't the aggressor; he was the victim."

Kelly had destroyed the case for the young prosecutor. The next evening, while eating dinner at his favorite steakhouse, Angie Callahan approached his table.

The detective lowered his steak knife, reached for his napkin, and smiled. "Counselor, how are you? Can I buy you drink?" Seeing the young attorney hesitating, he stood and pulled out a chair, hoping she would accept his invitation.

She did.

"I don't know if I should be consorting with the enemy," the young prosecutor said.

"I'm not your enemy, Angie. I just tell the truth as I see it. You wouldn't want an innocent man to serve time for a crime he didn't commit, would you?"

"No, I wouldn't, and it wasn't your fault that I lost my center on the case. I made the rookie mistake every attorney is warned about in Law School 101, never to ask—"

"A question to which you don't know the answer," Mike interrupted. "I have to say, Angie, when you asked the question, I almost laughed and was screaming inside—howling. 'Oh no,' I thought, 'how could this gorgeous woman ask such a dumb question?'"

"I must admit it was humiliating, and when I saw the judge lower his head, I knew the case was doomed. So you think that I'm gorgeous, do you?"

"I was smitten the first time that I testified for you when you nailed that low-life we put away. I was going to call and ask you to dinner, but I thought you'd blow me off."

"I didn't figure you to be someone who surrendered so easily," the young attorney said, opening the door of opportunity.

The detective wasted no time. "Well, let's start here. What's your flavor—steak or fish?" Kelly asked.

"I've always been a meat-eater." She reached for Mike's fork and stabbed a slice from his dish.

The next morning, the young prosecutor turned from her side of the bed and saw that Kelly was still asleep. She held her head and mumbled her chagrin. She slipped out of the covers, picking up her clothing on her way to the bathroom. She dressed and then placed a note on the night table before leaving.

Forty-five minutes later, Mike read the folded paper and smiled. It said, "Detective, I found your testimony intriguing and would like to clarify some points of our interaction. Call me."

The next day, while sitting at his desk, Mike twirled a small paper parasol, a reminder of the intimacy he had shared with the young district attorney. The ringing of his phone shattered the image of his intense experience with the woman he intended to get better acquainted with.

The two dated over the next six months, and it seemed like a match that would endure. Both were in careers that required independence of time constraints and not having to respond when necessity required a change of plans.

Angie and Mike were having dinner at the restaurant where they had their first connection. The waiter delivered the planned bottle of champagne and two glasses. The cork was popped and the wine poured. Angie did not anticipate what would follow. Mike reached for the box in his inside jacket pocket and opened it to show her the ring. Before he could utter a word, Angie stood from her chair.

Mike was bewildered, but Angie put both hands on Kelly's face and planted a kiss on his lips, showing her acceptance of his proposal. The restaurant patrons applauded in unison.

The next couple of years were content for the detective and the young prosecutor, but soon, the stress of their jobs began to have an impact on the relationship. It eroded when Mike's pursuit of Billy John Pratt intensified. It was the first marriage for Angie and the third for Kelly. He had been through the trials and tribulations with women who couldn't adjust to his marriage of the job; still, he thought it would be different this time.

But his wife's expectations clashed with his obsession, his determination to capture the felon who had become the crown of thorns in his life.

The final provocation occurred in a small fishing hamlet meant to reignite the marriage of the detective and the attorney. Instead, it crystallized the need for Angie to move on and for Mike to resolve an outcome—the killing of Billy John Pratt.

Death in Venezuela

Several thousand miles away, Billy had addressed the problem at hand. He decided to provide Rachael with enough information for her to decide whether to stay in Venezuela or leave for a destination unknown that, more than likely, was temporary.

With unrestrained tears, she shared her feelings within her heart; she wanted to be with him, wherever the destination. But her pregnancy, the future dependency of her mother, and raising a child with the uncertainty of permanence would be too much of a burden to endure. Rachael admitted her fear of Moises Husan. Before Billy left the country, he tranquilized her concerns, giving his promise that the extortionist would not be a threat to her in the future, though he gave no explanation.

In the dead of night, Billy left the apartment with nothing more than a duffel bag. The next morning, Moises didn't report for work; his body was discovered in his apartment two days later. His penis had been detached and stuffed in his mouth. His heart had been ripped from his chest and fed to his dog, remains left unfinished.

It was exceedingly brutal, an atrocious attack, intended to exact a penalty for the disrespect shown toward the assailant's woman.

Billy was in hiding for two days and then was hired as a hand on a freighter bound for Libya. It would be the last country for which he would depart.

When the police questioned Rachael on her man's whereabouts, they briefed her on his murderous past; like Gabrielle, she was overwhelmed.

Rachael was fired from the oil company and forced to live with her mother. She was resigned to giving birth to her child and finding a source of revenue, even if it meant returning to her previous life.

The Chase Continues

Detective Kelly was renewed and vowed to catch the elusive Pratt and bring him to justice. He continued to receive the support of his commander and the chief of detectives. Mike concluded that the ex-priest wouldn't remain in South America, now that his history had been exposed throughout the continent. He also dismissed his returning to the United States, which left Europe, the Middle East, and Africa in the detective's sights. He mulled over the possibilities, exploring those countries without extradition treaties with the United States. Europe was immediately eliminated, as the story of Billy's exploits was fodder for the Western and Eastern European countries. That left Africa and the Middle East, destinations that did not take kindly to those who murdered their citizens.

It was a staggering undertaking, one that required complete support from his superiors. It was a task for a younger man, not for one whose battle scars cried for sipping piña coladas under the palm trees of Florida or California. He was given eight months to bring the killer to justice; then he'd have to allow the FBI to continue their pursuit, as Billy John Pratt had been on their Ten Most Wanted list for several years. It was 2010, and the bureau was no closer to capturing their man than when the felon initially made the list.

It was a cold Thursday in February when Kelly's phone rang. On the line was an agent from the Federal Bureau of Investigation, Christopher Dodd. Mike was finally going to get the support he desperately needed, and the young FBI agent would be the reinforcement tonic for the frustrated detective.

Chapter 19

Survive or Die

THE MAN WHO DISEMBARKED in Tripoli was no stranger to survival in foreign ports. The name on his passport was Michael Porter. He came ashore and was walking down the gangway when he observed a boy of about seven break away from his mother's grasp and fall into the water between the dock and ship. His mother cried out for help. Billy dove from the gangway into the narrow space of the water and grabbed hold of the boy. He and the lad escaped being crushed between the ship and the dock, and both were hoisted from the water by his shipmates, who congratulated Billy for his heroics.

The boy's mother and father, surrounded by armed guards, approached the man who saved their son's life. They thanked him for his bravery. The father was a prince in the constitutional monarchy of the country.

"May I know your name, sir?" asked the forty-two year-old member of the royal family.

"My name is Michael Porter," said the fugitive, with water dripping from his body.

The prince snapped an order in Arabic, and a guard immediately took his ankle-length tunic from his body and gave it to Billy so he could dry himself.

"Where are you residing, Mr. Porter?" asked the prince.

"Sir, I haven't made arrangements yet."

"My wife and I would be honored if you would allow us the pleasure of providing accommodations for you."

"Thank you, but on one condition," he said.

The prince taken aback. "And what would that be, sir?"

"That the honor would be mine for your gracious offer."

The prince placed his arm around the shoulders of the man who had saved the young royal from certain death, followed by a broad smile.

The prince and the ex-priest engaged in conversation during the forty-five-minute drive from Tripoli to the palace. The royal wanted to know about the man he'd invited to his home. As Billy responded to his questions, the prince weighed his words, attempting to determine if the stranger was the messenger of his nightly prayers.

It was dusk when they arrived at the palace. Billy was shown to his quarters and was told that dinner would be within the hour. After bathing, he dressed and stood on the balcony, observing the vast expanse of the property and musing over his good fortune. For a brief moment, he questioned his belief in a deity. Why would God provide a safe haven for one who had violated his commandment of "Thou shall not kill"? He speculated that perhaps it was a window of redemption; the saving of a boy was akin to the birth of a deliverer. His reflection was interrupted when he was summoned to dinner. He removed his shoes before approaching the table.

Michael Porter was warmly greeted by members of the royal family, and several expressed their gratitude for saving the young prince. When he was seated, a bowl of perfumed water was passed around the table, and each person dipped three fingers as a ritual of cleansing before the meal. The table was filled with an array of food—lamb soup, meats, pasta, and sweet tea. The conversation was casual and upbeat; they spoke English in honor of their guest. After dinner, the prince and his wife sat with Michael to discuss a proposal.

"Mr. Porter, from our brief discussions, it's unmistakable that you're a man of education and refinement. You've also proven to be a man of courage and conviction, a rare trait that is admired. Our country is in political disarray, and we fear for our son's safety while attending school. He's afforded protection to and from the academy but not when he's in the building. Terrorist factions within our country are devoid of decency and are misguided in the teachings of Muhammad, the prophet of Allah. They bomb buildings filled with women and children and then celebrate their mass killing with praises to Allah.

"Our fear is your opportunity, Mr. Porter. My wife and I would like you to become our son's educator, here at the palace. Your compensation would be generous—$125,000, American. Your lodgings and food would be included. We hope you welcome our offer."

Billy needed no arm-twisting to accept the proposal. Prince Abdul and his wife showed genuine concern for their son's welfare, and what better place to burrow in than a royal house?

FBI in Boston

Detective Kelly was able to narrow Billy's escape route to a freighter bound for the African continent, but the country of destination was still unclear. His request for the ship's manifest was rebuked. There were sixteen countries in Western Africa and seven in North Africa. The question was, which of those was the freighter's destination, and where did Billy go when he went ashore.

It was an expansive search, and his commander's cooperation was waning. Resources were devoted to ongoing domestic cases, and the chief reminded him that he was on a short leash of eight months to close the case.

But he had an ally in FBI agent Chris Dodd, who also was on a crusade to capture the elusive killer.

Dodd and Kelly pooled their resources. They listed all ports of entry on the west, north, and east coast of Africa, eliminating those that didn't accommodate large freighters. The remaining ports spanned from the Ivory Coast to South Africa on the west coast, to Egypt, Libya, and Morocco in the north. They could narrow the search if the manifest of the freighter, SS *Bismist* was made available, but the ship owner was inaccessible. They were determined to find the freighter's port of entry and began calling every port on the African coast, hoping to locate the ship.

"Something doesn't add up," said Dodd. "All ships must be registered, and manifests listing cargo, passengers, and crew must be available to customs agents and other officials. Perhaps we're being stonewalled because the cargo of the *Bismist* didn't conform to its registry."

"Doesn't a ship's flag point to the identity of the owner?" Kelly asked.

"No, not necessarily. In fact, most ships are mere carriers of cargo owned by other countries."

"Chris, I have to admit that this bullshit chase is starting to wear me down. As much as I hate to let this guy get away, the consequences of pursuing him are pervasive. I've lost wives, girlfriends, partners, and time to the job." Kelly lowered his head in dejection.

"I know what the both of us need—a good meal and some hard liquor. Let's ditch this place and lighten the mood," suggested Dodd.

The two left the precinct and drove to a celebrated steakhouse.

"Chris, what made you join the bureau?" Mike asked, sipping on his bourbon.

"It's a family history, and I didn't want to break the chain. My grandfather and father were both in the bureau, so naturally, I followed the tradition. When I graduated law school, I applied for the job. What made you decide to be a cop?"

"Somewhat the same. My dad was on the force and a gold shield. It just seemed the road to follow," said the detective.

The waiter then asked for their orders.

"I hear you lost two partners to this bastard," Dodd said.

"Chris, in my years on the force and the hundreds of dirtbags collared, I've never been scratched, and none of my partners was shot. Now, at the twilight of my career, two are killed by this back-stabbing son of a bitch." Mike didn't want to mention his intimate relationship with Maggie, though he was still mindful of the violent event.

"I feel for you, Mike. I've never been in that position and hope never to experience that kind of heartbreak." Chris suspected a personal relationship between Mike and Maggie, as Kelly's visual communication was revealing.

The two law enforcement agents ripped into their steaks while discussing possible approaches to narrowing the search for the elusive killer. They were on the same wavelength, and a respect was developing between the two—possibly a friendship in the making. Chris revealed he was twice divorced and had two children from the damaged relationships. He was forty-four, younger than his counterpart, and in good shape. He was pleasing in appearance at a chiseled six-foot one. His complexion was fair, showing his Irish heritage. His eyes were blue, and his hair was red.

After dinner, they agreed to resume their search in the morning. Just as they rose to leave, Mike was startled to see Angie enter the restaurant with a man by her side. It was inevitable that they would cross paths; this was the restaurant where he had first proposed marriage to the assistant prosecutor.

"Hello, Mike."

"Angie."

"This is my fiancé, Doug Saunders."

"Doug Saunders—aren't you the new district attorney?" asked Kelly, with a wry smile.

"Why, yes, I am."

"Nice seeing you both," Mike said. He abruptly walked past them, telling Dodd, "Don't ask."

Kelly reckoned that Angie had climbed the ladder.

At the Palace in Libya

"Good morning, Mr. Porter. I hope you don't mind if I attend the first session of my son's education with you." said the mother of Tareq, the seven-year-old, who was clutching his mother's cloak.

"Not at all. I believe it's in both our interests," Billy responded.

The mother nodded her approval, as the two had previously discussed her son's preferences and her husband's expectations. Billy was also reminded of their Muslim heritage and the prince's required prayer five times daily, called the *salat*.

"The first thing we have do, Tareq, is for you and me to make each other's acquaintance," said Mr. Porter, squatting to the boy's line of vision and attempting to set a tone.

The shy seven-year-old was still clinging to his mother.

"Tareq, when I was a boy your age, I could stay in this position forever, but now it's very uncomfortable to do so for very long. So with your permission, may I sit on the floor while I introduce myself?"

The boy nodded the go-ahead. Billy continued to try to put Tareq at ease, asking if he liked sports and which he favored; he already knew the answer. He asked if the boy liked arts-and-crafts projects and what his favorite subjects were. Before long, they were engaged in meaningful dialogue. The young student was at ease with the man who'd saved his life and no longer clutched his mother's tunic.

Billy stood and then placed two chairs ten feet apart. He reached into a box behind his desk and retrieved a soccer ball, placing it twenty feet in front of the chairs. The boy's mother had indicated soccer was his favorite activity, and Billy challenged Tareq to kick the ball past him and between the two chairs. Without hesitation, the young prince's familiarity with soccer became evident. The ball whizzed by his instructor and between the two chairs, not just once but in every attempt, which astounded his new mentor.

Before long, Tareq was sitting in a chair while his teacher placed questions on the blackboard for discussion. His mother was pleased by the promising beginning.

Billy dined with the family each evening, and Tareq's father noticed the budding relationship between his son and the instructor. The boy no longer sat at his father's side but next to Mr. Porter. At first, the prince and his wife were pleased that their son had forged a close bond with his instructor. But over time, the father became envious of the relationship and expected his son to remember his kinship.

"Abdul, the boy is happy. Wasn't that your treasured wish?" his wife asked.

"Yes, Sarah, I'm pleased with the boy's transition, but Tareq seems engrossed with Mr. Porter and has little time for his parents."

"Perhaps, my husband, if you occasionally attend his instruction time, you would feel better, and he would see your genuine interest in his development." Sarah placed her arm around her bruised husband.

Over the next three days, the prince attended his son's classes and appreciated the direction of his education. The three interacted by playing an occasional game of soccer during rest period.

"Tareq, Mr. Porter tells me that you're doing exceedingly well in your studies. I'm proud of you, my son."

"Thank you, Father. I have something for you," said the young prince, reaching into his desk.

When the price saw his son's gift, tears welled in his eyes. Tareq had drawn a picture of the two of them, standing side-by-side. On the bottom of the picture, he had written, "I love my father." The drawing was impressive for a seven-year-old and showed a budding gift that hadn't blossomed before his relationship with his mentor.

The young boy inspired Billy, who had deserted a family of three and a girlfriend pregnant with his child. His sense of family was resuscitated in the process of educating the young prince. He had little time for his two boys in Brazil, as running the ranch and his venture into politics had sapped his good intentions. He was no longer the killer of those who opposed his fast lane of life; he had emotionally bonded with the boy and was willing to do whatever necessary to protect the young prince.

On the first Friday of April, Billy received permission to take the young prince to town, changing the academia routine for a day of frivolity. It was a brisk day, as the temperature was a mere fifty-eight degrees. Billy and the prince were driven to town by a royal bodyguard. The car was parked, and the three started their journey through the expansive market, with vendors hawking their goods along the way. The young prince's eyes widened when they passed a vendor selling pizza. Billy bought three slices and sodas for the prince, his bodyguard, and him. They were huddled at an outdoor table, fighting the cool temperatures while enjoying their pizza, when a man approached with a handgun and aimed his weapon at the young prince. Billy reacted instinctively, shielding the boy with his body, two bullets penetrating his back before the would-be assassin was gunned down by the royal's bodyguard.

The news of the attempted assassination of the young prince and the heroics of his American instructor was the news of the day, but it was publicity that Billy did not favor. The bullets had missed critical organs, and the surgery to remove the fragmented projectiles was successful. He was hospitalized for a week, and upon his return to the palace, he was hailed for his courage in saving the prince for the second time.

Prince Abdul asked to speak to the instructor in the privacy of his study.

"Mr. Porter, words cannot express my gratitude for what you did at the marketplace. You're quite a remarkable man to lay your life down for my son. What makes you do such a thing?" the prince asked.

Billy hesitated before answering. "Prince Abdul, when you live in the jungle of life, you learn to survive, or you die. We live in a labyrinth of confusion, where people with puzzling agendas attempt to take the life of your son. What would the death of a young boy accomplish? What kind of God do they think would sanction that kind of treachery?"

The knotty question elicited a resigned response. "My country and my father are under siege by radical factions. Their attempt on my son's life was a message— that they will stop at nothing to accomplish their agenda, which is overthrowing the monarchy."

The prince had never questioned the background of the man hired as his son's instructor. But his curiosity was rising above his restraint. Who was this refined man who worked as a common hand on a freighter with a worldly education and the courage of a bold warrior? He finally asked the question.

"I see only two reasons for a man to exile himself from his country, Mr. Porter. He's either a wanted man or one whose desperation triggers a desire to escape from himself—a repentance, if you will, for sins of the past. Which is it, Mr. Porter?"

"Prince Abdul, there are times when certain things are better left unsaid, and I ask that you respect that this is one of those times." Billy eyeballed the prince, realizing that his sanctuary might be at an end.

"I don't always see eye-to-eye with my father, Mr. Porter, and several are issues better left unsaid between us, so I do empathize and respect your privacy. Please know this: I will always be indebted to the man I wish to acknowledge as one who has shown an unwavering devotion to our son. Please accept my hand in friendship, Mr. Porter."

The relationship between the royal family and the man they knew as Michael Porter blossomed over the next several weeks.

The prince turned eight in June. Tareq was highly intelligent and an eager learner of Western culture. He wanted to know the interests of American children his age. He didn't have the benefit of interacting with other children, a damaging aspect of homeschooling. One morning, when he reported for his daily education, his instructor noticed a change in the young boy's deportment. He was unusually quiet and sullen. When Billy asked him about it, the prince admitted he was unhappy because he didn't share experiences with other children.

At the end of the week, Billy approached Prince Abdul and his wife to relate his concerns for the lack of social interaction between their son and other children his age. On Monday morning, when Tareq came to class, his eyes widened; he was astonished to see five other children in attendance. The prince and his wife had listened to Billy's concerns and acted promptly, inviting close friends to have their children participate in the homeschooling program. The prince provided transportation to and from the palace and increased Billy's salary to reflect his new responsibilities.

One day after class, the young prince and Billy were sitting on a bench overlooking the palace gardens. Tareq turned to his mentor and asked a knotty question that Billy hesitated to answer.

"Mr. Porter, do you have children?"

It was an innocent inquiry, but Billy looked to the sky, trying to piece together an answer that wouldn't elicit further probing of his past.

"No, Tareq, I don't have children, but if I did, I would wish they were as handsome and bright as you."

The answer evoked a broad smile from the boy. Billy's response was measured but also pierced his defensive veil of bravado. Although he'd removed himself from his past, he indeed missed Gabino and Diego; he longed to see his boys. The idea of their experiencing life without a father was calamitous, even for the prolific killer. He hadn't been particularly close with his own father, but he had been there until Billy entered the seminary.

Billy gazed at the horizon and reflected upon the direction of his life, wondering how it all went wrong. He cupped his head in his hands, wishing that past misdeeds could magically melt away and that he could have a new beginning. *Was Gabrielle right?* he thought. *Is absolution possible if I confess and repent?* His reflections tormented him, and he visualized the devil's agents hovering in the shadows, their talons ready to rip into his flesh.

"Mr. Porter, are you all right?" Tareq asked, concerned about his trusted teacher.

The ex-priest snapped himself from the claws of despair. "Yes, son, I'm just fine," he said. "I think it's time for a bite of lunch." He placed his arm around the boy, and they walked together to the kitchen, unaware that a major mishap was about to rock Billy's world.

Chapter 20

Unexpected Crisis

D ETECTIVE KELLY AND FBI agent Christopher Dodd had narrowed the
scope of their investigation. They were successful in acquiring the manifest
of the freighter, SS *Bismist*. They reviewed the names of the crew, but Billy
John Pratt wasn't among those listed, nor was anyone with the known aliases
used by the killer. They realized that any member of the crew could be the man
they were hunting.

The ship had disembarked cargo in four different ports. The question was,
which of the four ports did their felon choose for his escape? It still had the
two lawmen in a vicious circle, as all four possibilities were escape routes to
neighboring countries.

Kelly favored the ports in Nigeria and Libya, while Dodd favored Morocco
and Cairo. It was a frustrating task with limited manpower and resources. But
now that the scope had been narrowed, they agreed to contact the harbormaster
of each country and hope for a lucky break. From Boston, there was a six-hour
time difference to Morocco and Nigeria and seven hours to Egypt and Libya.

It was early September when they made the first inquiry to the harbormasters
of Nigeria and Morocco. Both said there was no indication that anyone fitting
Billy Pratt's description had disembarked from the *Bismist*. There also was
nothing forthcoming from the officials in charge of the remaining ports in
Morocco and Libya.

They were back to square one, with scant hope of meeting the deadline set
by their superiors.

"Chris, I don't have the goddamned foggiest idea where to turn from here," Kelly snapped, his frustration mounting.

Dodd nodded his agreement. "I know the feeling, but we can't surrender—not just yet. The one thing the job has taught me over the years is that the smallest details can crack a case wide open. Perhaps we're missing a footprint, a triviality located in a bigger picture. Let's go over this again." Dodd stood and began pacing the room. "We have a list of the ship's crew, and we verified that the freighter anchored in the ports of four countries. The harbormasters verified that none of the crew fit the description of our perp."

"Chris, is it possible that the harbormasters we spoke to are new to the job or weren't on duty when the freighter anchored?" Kelly asked.

"What do you mean?"

"Consider this: what job requires someone to be there twenty-four/seven? We work shifts, so why not harbormasters?"

They looked at each other and then sprang to the phones. Two of the four harbormasters weren't on duty when the *Bismist* anchored. One had retired, and the other, from Tripoli, was on vacation and wouldn't return for another week. It would be a difficult wait for the Boston cop and the FBI agent.

Back in Libya

"Mr. Porter, the political situation in my country is reaching a turning point, and I fear for the safety of my family," Prince Abdul said. "I'm informing you, as you could become a casualty in a battle that's not your conflict. I can no longer guarantee your safety in a clash that might occur at any time. The situation is very fluid. My father is on the battlefield as we speak."

"What's the opposition's issue?" Billy asked.

"The concept of a constitutional monarchy has been a source of contention for many years, with different political factions pushing for change and governmental reform, but in reality, they're gangsters with a different spin. I'll fully understand if you wish to take your leave, Mr. Porter."

"Prince Abdul, are you taking your family from the compound?"

"Not at this time, but that's not to say it won't occur tomorrow or the next day."

"I appreciate the heads-up, but I'm not a man to run from a fight that I believe in, and it's not a political belief; your son is special to me. He's given to me as much as I have to him. You once indirectly asked why I abandoned my country, and you speculated there might be one of two reasons: to avoid capture from the authorities or to escape the demons of past sins. I didn't answer then, and I don't intend to now, but be aware, that when I'm cornered, my survival instincts kick in. With that, I ask that you provide weapons for me to protect your only child and my worthless life."

The prince was startled by the teacher's remark.

The next day, instruction continued in a routine fashion—except that Billy was provided the protection he requested. Hidden in the closet was an AK-47 assault rifle with ample ammunition and two Glock automatic pistols. The prince's personal bodyguard sat at the rear of the room. It was a tense environment for the royal family as well as the children, who suspected that the appearance of the prince's bodyguard foreshadowed a hidden danger.

A week passed without incident, but the prince no longer allowed the other children to be included with his son's instruction. The burden of protection was too great if there was an attack, it could obstruct his son's safety.

Kelly in Boston

"Mike, get this—I called the harbormaster of Tripoli, the guy who was on vacation. He verified that our man disembarked from the *Bismist*. And you're not going to believe this—the ex-priest dove into the harbor to save some kid, and he turned out to be part of the royal family."

Kelly grinned from ear to ear and slapped his desk. "Son of a bitch, son of a bitch! Chris, we've got the bastard."

"Don't be hasty; there's no extradition treaty with Libya and the country's on the verge of civil war. We don't know if he's on the run to neighboring countries or still in Libya," said Chris.

"But we have a point of reference. How about the family of the kid he saved? Maybe they can give us a direction and a time of reference," Kelly suggested.

Chris picked up the phone. "I'll call the harbormaster and ask if he can provide information on the family."

The harbormaster gave the FBI agent more than he bargained for. He explained that the man who saved the prince from drowning, also saved him again during an attempted assassination, when he shielded the prince with his own body, resulting in his being shot twice.

The FBI agent was astonished, as was Kelly.

"You're a fugitive, and then you save a prince and lived with the royal family as a teacher," Chris said. "I thought I'd heard it all, but this takes the cake."

"Yeah, you think that's astonishing? How about becoming the governor of the largest city in Brazil, getting married to a prominent rancher's daughter, and becoming a father of three kids? This guy is one for the books. Someone will come along and write a book that becomes a best-seller by covering this killer's exploits."

"I hear you, Mike. But you almost have to admire his tenacity."

"Enough of the homage. Why don't you ask your field director to make contact with the royal family to determine if Pratt is living in the palace?" Kelly proposed.

"I can do that. If we can't extradite him, we can at least make his life full of misery," Dodd said triumphantly.

At the Palace

"Mr. Porter, we received a communication today from a station chief of the FBI," the prince said, seeming anxious. "He believes you fit the description of a person who has committed several murders in the United States and other countries. I told my diplomatic minister there must be a mistake. The Michael Porter we are housing cannot be the man they describe. Your government agency is forwarding a series of photographs to the palace."

Billy was taken by surprise, but the quick-witted killer smiled and then calmly made the case for mistaken identity. He convinced the prince that governments had incarcerated innocent people before and would continue to do so with misguided information.

"They're barking up the wrong tree, my friend. They may send photos of someone who may or may not have a resemblance to me, but I'm not their person of interest."

The prince accepted Billy's explanation. He assumed it was true, and he was relieved that his son's instructor wasn't a potential menace to his family. There were more menacing dangers for the prince to cope with.

His father had communicated that the battle against those who opposed the monarchy was in peril. He advised the prince to make plans for the safety of his family; the situation was grave.

It was Friday evening. Billy needed to relieve the tension created by the prince's warning. He went into town and visited the red-light district. It had been several months since his last encounter with a woman. He spent much of the evening entertaining the two ladies he hired to provide physical relief and consolation.

He lay in bed with his arms folded behind his head, staring at the rotating blades of the fan; both women were sound asleep. His thoughts flashed back to his childhood, and he wondered if a single event had sealed his fate. His mind was recasting the past to a life of propriety and importance. *After all, I did become a governor*, he thought. *Perhaps I could have had greatness in politics.* His thoughts of fame continued …

"Mr. President, the leaders of the free world are awaiting your counsel."

"Doctor, you've been awarded the Nobel Prize for your cure of cancer."

"General, the men await your orders."

Billy's expression turned from exultation to sorrow. His life had been defined; he was a murderer, a violator of human dignity. He retrieved the pistol from beneath the pillow and placed it to his temple. The father of four was in the depths of desperation and remorse. He cocked the gun and squeezed his eyes shut as his finger approached the trigger.

His impulse of ending his life came to an abrupt halt when the door to his room came crashing to the floor. Two thieves approached, with swords raised. Billy shot both dead within a whisper of time. He leaped from his bed, stepping over the lifeless bodies, as the two women screamed, frightened for their lives. He quickly dressed and raced past the curious who had gathered outside the room.

Billy leaped into the jeep and drove back to the palace, concerned that the attempted robbery indicated a breakdown of civil obedience. Three miles before reaching his destination, he approached what appeared to be a checkpoint on the road—two cars blocked the way, and three armed men signaled for him to slow down. He reached for his semiautomatic Glock, concealing it in his belt behind his back. Two armed men, dressed in khakis, approached his car. They demanded he step out from the vehicle; one man pointed his rifle at Billy. They asked for his passport, which he had left at the palace, but he explained that he was the instructor of Prince Abdul's son.

The three men huddled in what appeared to be a sinister discussion, and one of them slowly unclipped the holster to his pistol. When he suddenly unholstered the gun, Billy dove behind the jeep and opened fire, killing the three men. He searched the bodies, looking for identification, and extracted plastic-covered tags. Then he proceeded to the palace, speculating that the royals were in trouble and that the prince had more to be concerned about than the arrival of the FBI photos. He began framing a response to the photos that were sure to be waiting for him at the palace.

"Mr. Porter, the political situation is deteriorating by the hour, and for your own safety, I suggest you stay within the palace compound," warned the prince after Billy gave his account of the recent events. "You say the men who confronted you were three miles from the palace?"

"Yes, Prince Abdul. I took these tags from the bodies,"

The prince inspected the identities of the men. "These thugs are part of the opposition that is threatening the monarchy. My father has been battling them for years."

His wife entered the room, with another person by her side. "Forgive the interruption, my husband. My sister Nada has arrived and wishes to thank you for providing her sanctuary at the palace." She turned to Billy. "Mr. Porter, pardon my rudeness; may I present my sister, Nada."

Sarah's twenty-five-year-old sister was stunning and captivated Billy's imagination.

The prince took notice and pulled the teacher aside. "The FBI photos haven't arrived. Communications to the palace have been interrupted."

Prince Abdul placed his confidence in the man who twice had saved his son from certain death, and he attached little weight to the accusation made by the American authorities. He considered Billy a warrior, not by title but by raw inner courage in the time of crisis—something most professed to have within their adventurous characters but were bankrupt when given the opportunity to demonstrate.

"The palace could be under siege at any time," the prince confided to Billy. "I urge you to carry on with your duties. Remain calm but alert, and be ready to vacate the palace when necessary. I have made arrangements for my family to flee to a neighboring country—and you are included in that plan."

It was difficult to restore a sense of normality in the palace while communications to the outside world were impeded, but Billy continued to train the young prince. One morning, an unexpected visitor listened from behind a column of the palace. Billy waved to the inquisitive aunt, suggesting that she sit next to her nephew. Although Libya was a Muslim country, there was no imposed dress code for women. The slender beauty was dressed in a long-sleeved cotton dress. It was black and embellished with a colorful necklace and lace collar; three V-shaped designs adorned the front of the dress. She wasn't wearing the traditional hijab around her head and face, so her satiny skin and seductive eyes were exposed.

Nada was intrigued with Mr. Porter's teachings and soon began to ask questions that showed her unfamiliarity with Western culture—subject matter approved by the royal family. Before long, the two were taking walks in the palace gardens and discussing a variety of topics.

They were sitting on a bench when Billy's desire to know more about Nada reached a point of boldness. He asked if she ever had been married or engaged, and her response astonished the ex-priest. She lowered her head, embarrassed about the coming disclosure.

Billy reached for her hand. "You have nothing to be ashamed of in being virtuous," he said, "That is a symbol of pureness and respect."

But she went further, wanting to know what the experience of intimacy invoked in an individual. The discussion was arousing Billy, and his imagination expanded to his being in the bedroom with the young woman. He presumed that an activity she could relate to would answer her question. Tactfully, he asked how she felt when pleasuring herself.

Nada blushed, appreciating the directness of the question, and then startled Billy with her response. "It is a sin, according to Muslim law, to engage in self-pleasuring." Her explanation was like a chicken innocently strolling into the den of a fox, and Billy was the willing Zen master who retreated to his room with Nada.

The Muslim woman's first experience of sexual intercourse was beyond her expectations. There was no bleeding or pain, as she had heard in her teenage years; there was only pure, unadulterated pleasure. Her only regret was that she had abstained for so many years from the experience. She indulged in things she hadn't envisioned and commanded more from the man who introduced her to the world of pleasure. Her stamina amazed the debauchery-driven ex-priest. Her firsthand knowledge made her aware in the limitations of multiple orgasms by men, commanding a sense of superiority when engaging in sexual pleasures.

"You're simply amazing, Nada," Billy said, exhausted and gasping for air.

"Did I please you?" she asked, placing a hand on the chest of her first lover.

"For a woman who never had experienced the joy of lovemaking, I'd give you a grade of a hundred-percent."

Billy's words authenticated the captivated joy within the depths of her chamber. They moved toward each other until their bodies joined, igniting their primeval instincts.

The next morning, when all were in attendance for breakfast, Sarah noticed a radiant glow in her sister. She tapped her husband's elbow and nodded in Nada's direction.

The prince wasn't amused, nor did he sanction the relationship; he demanded that Porter meet with him, suspecting a social betrayal by the man he welcomed in his home.

"Mr. Porter, your function at the palace is instructing our son. It does not extend to personal relationships with members of the royal family. I dare not ask how far this edict has been violated, but you will restrict your activities to your employment. This isn't a request, Mr. Porter."

"Prince Abdul, let me get clarification. Are you saying it's acceptable that I save your son from certain death, but I'm not good enough to socialize with your sister-in-law?" Billy asked, driving his point into the face of the royal.

"Nada is Muslim and will marry another royal, another Muslim. That's the way of our country."

"And if she decides otherwise?"

"She has no voice in the matter, and you—of all people—should know the ways of our country, or have you forgotten our generosity, Mr. Billy John Pratt?"

Billy was unnerved by the prince's stunning words. The royal then disclosed that the FBI photos had been transmitted and unquestionably showed Billy as the fugitive wanted for multiple murders.

"What has kept you from exposing my identity?" Billy asked—but the answer became clear to the ex-priest before the prince could answer. The monarch's situation was tenuous, and plans for abandoning the palace were in place. The prince had determined that a man of Billy's combatant mentality, along with his fondness for Tareq, was an asset if the palace came under siege.

"So it wasn't out of gratitude or friendship that you withheld my identity but for your greedy backup plan," Billy sniped.

"You shouldn't throw rocks at the glass house that provided you shelter and refuge. I ask you … is my greed more treacherous than your past sins, Billy? What we do is for survival, and my family is in great peril. I suggest we dismiss the past and work in collaboration—for the well-being of us both."

"It would be easy for me to go, leaving you to resolve your own problems, but

I have two reasons for staying and allowing time to determine our fates. You do need me around, but I'll stay on my own terms and not what you dictate—that includes continuing Tareq's education and seeing Nada whenever she wishes. If we can't agree, then I'll leave the palace within five minutes. Don't think for a moment that my survival hasn't been predicated upon my own passage out of this country." Billy had drawn his line in the sand and now waited for the royal's response.

"You're a man on the run, Billy. Consider what that means for my sister-in-law. You may be smitten, and she as well, but can you tell me what tomorrow may bring? She's now deflowered and no longer fit for a Muslim husband; it's our tradition. I understand you've left behind a family and a pregnant woman. Is that what you want for Nada?"

"Prince Abdul, can you be sure what tomorrow will bring for you and your family? Nada brings me peace and comfort, something every man desires in a woman. You and I—we're on equal terms. Neither of us can be sure what may lie ahead, but we're both prepared for our fates."

"We aren't on equal footing, Billy. I'm not an international criminal wanted for murder."

"This palace you live in is a birthright because of your father. I ask you: how did he become ruler? I'm sure it wasn't by a mandate from the people. Your father is in the battle of his life, trying to preserve what you call the monarchy. Others call it a dictatorship, and in that form of rule, people are killed in order to maintain power. So please, Prince Abdul, don't hide from the truth."

The onetime relationship of trust between the prince and Billy clearly had deteriorated. The royal was angered that his wife's sister had been violated. That it might have been consensual was immaterial; she was no longer fit to marry another royal or a Muslim. If the political circumstances had been different, the prince would have had Billy beheaded and Nada beaten and then sold into slavery. There was now a questionable and narrow complicity between the royal and the ex-priest.

"It seems we're at an impasse, and circumstances dictate that we put aside our differences for the common good," said the prince. "I expect Tareq to continue his education, while you demonstrate propriety and discretion with my wife's sister. Be aware, Billy, if you should suddenly vanish in the night, you will have sealed Nada's fate." The prince's threat was clear: Nada was now the ward of her lover.

"Your sister has disgraced this house, Sarah. She's fornicated with a killer, a man with no future but with a certain destiny. You were responsible for her propriety. She's a worthless Muslim, unfit for marriage in our family."

"My husband, I've shamed you, and for that, I'm sorry. Nada is no longer a child and is responsible for her actions. I will honor whatever you propose."

"My hands are tied, and for the safety of our family, I must enter into an alliance with a murderer. I wish my father could sail to victory over his enemies. It would provide a clear picture of the future of our family," the prince moaned.

His wife left in dishonor and summoned her sister to the courtyard. "My sister, you have brought shame to our house and to me. You spread your legs for a non-Muslim, a murderer. You forever sealed your fate as well as mine."

"I'm sorry for you, sister, but not for me. I longed to be with a man, not to wait for someone else's approval and not my own. It's my body, and I alone determine what I can and cannot do with it, not some antiquated law or my sister's husband."

"Did you, for a moment in your lustful passion, consider the consequences to your sister?" Sarah asked. "Abdul has been faithful to one wife—me! Now, he has disavowed you and places blame for your fornication on your sister. He can take as many wives as he sees fit, and your selfish passion will result in my sharing the prince with others. I hate you for this and no longer consider you my sister. You will not dine at the same table or address my husband or son in discourse. Now, leave me before I beat you, as you deserve for your indiscretion."

Billy and Nada no longer shared the same dinner table with the royal family—Billy by choice; Nada by decree. They ate in his room, discussing the ramifications of their relationship.

"The many times I sat in your discussions with my nephew, I marveled at those lessons about Western culture and the freedoms enjoyed by its people. It had a profound influence in my reasoning. I rejoiced in the self-dignity of choosing what I wanted to be and not what others have declared me to be. For that and what I've experienced with you, I have no regrets."

"Nada, my future is vague and filled with dangers that could result in my death at any time. I make no allusions about the time we share and the destiny of our paths. All I know … is that I care for you a great deal and would gladly give my life for your safety."

"Let's partake of the moment; it can be a lifetime of joy with no regrets. My sister has told me about your past, and it has no meaning or purpose for what I feel in my heart."

The ex-priest was overwhelmed by his lover's posture and affection.

But he did not suspect that the dogged persistence of a Boston detective would disrupt his world.

Chapter 21
The Net Tightens

IT WAS OCTOBER, AND the deadline for capturing the infamous killer was near. Detective Mike Kelly and FBI agent Chris Dodd had found the needle in the haystack by identifying the country in which Billy John Pratt was encamped. They had forwarded the information to the palace but had not received a response. It was as if they were looking into a mirror, seeing the felon within their grasp, but reflected back to them was the image of Pratt, thumbing his nose in mockery.

Kelly was fifteen years older than his FBI agent counterpart and considering retirement. He was at a critical juncture in his career. If he didn't capture the felon he'd been stalking for years, his life history on the Boston police force would be forever scarred. He put his arm around Dodd's shoulder, thanking him for his efforts.

The FBI agent was mystified and taken aback. "What are you saying, Mike?" Dodd, looking confused, shrugged the detective's hand from his shoulder.

"It's over, Chris. We can't carry on trying to nail this bastard. He's beaten us as cops. We're out of time, and the authorities in Libya have their hands full of problems other than cooperating with American detectives in arresting a felon."

"But we're too close to give up now; it invalidates all of our efforts."

"Let's face reality. The bureau isn't going to send a contingent of agents to Libya to apprehend Pratt. No, if anything, it has to be covert. It's a one-man operation for someone with nothing to lose."

"Are you kidding me, Mike? What are you going to do—walk into the palace where he's holed up and show your badge, demanding that the prince surrender Pratt? Are you suicidal? Because that's what I'm hearing," barked the FBI agent.

"He killed two of my partners. I can't let that slide. Whatever it takes, I have to make a go of it. I'll be incompetent if I end my career on a clunker." Mike stood from his chair, fist-bumped the FBI agent, and then left for the commander's office. He asked if the captain could extend the deadline for capturing Pratt and was immediately rebuffed by his boss. There was a brief silence before the detective reached for his badge and gun and placed them on the captain's desk.

"What's this, Mike?"

"I'm done, Captain. If I can't resume the chase with the blessing of my ranking officers, then I'll go it alone."

"Mike, be sensible. In a month, it will go away and become another cold case in our files. Why end your career like this?"

"As long as I take a breath, it will never be over, Captain. It's under my skin and is a perpetual reminder that Pratt murdered two of my partners."

"And you think going to a hostile country and getting yourself killed will bring them back?"

"You're not in my shoes, Captain, so I don't expect you to see through my eyes."

"Mike, when you walk out that door, you're a private citizen with no backup. If you get in a jam in Libya, there's no lifeline for you."

"I understand, Captain. Thanks for the good fight." Kelly shook the commander's hand and left the office.

Five Days Later

"May I see your passport?" the customs agent said. When Mike handed it to the agent, he asked, "What is the purpose of your visit, Mr. Kelly?"

"Vacation," Mike responded.

"It's very unusual for an American to be vacationing in our country, sir."

"My father married a woman from Libya, and I'm curious about my heritage."

"She was a Muslim?"

"Yes."

"How did they meet?"

"My father worked for a California-based oil company and met my mother in your country. One thing led to another, and I'm the result."

"How long are you staying in our beautiful country, Mr. Kelly?"

"Five days or less."

"Where are you staying?"

"At the Corinthia in Tripoli."

"A fine choice. Enjoy your stay, Mr. Kelly," said the agent.

Mike thanked the man and headed for the taxi stand.

After checking into the hotel, Mike ate dinner and then went to the gift shop. He purchased sundry items, along with an essential one—a map of the surrounding area, which included the palace of Prince Abdul.

"Sarah, word has come that my father has been killed, assassinated by the barbarians who wish to overthrow the monarchy. It's no longer safe to remain at the palace. Prepare our son to leave within the next two hours; pack only essentials," the prince said.

But then, a series of shots rang out, followed by chilling screams.

"Where's Nada?" the prince asked with a sense of urgency.

"She left the palace with the infidel some hours ago," Sarah cried, rushing away to locate her son.

Billy looked at the menu and then at Nada, yielding the process to her. She ordered a salad, seafood with a rice dish, and sweet tea—alcohol was banned in Libya. They were enjoying the ambiance of the Corinthia Hotel, which was less then an hour's drive from the palace. Their first course arrived; the salad included a sprinkling of dates and nuts. They were engaged in conversation when Mike Kelly did a double-take when exiting the gift shop.

Kelly couldn't believe that Lady Luck had turned in his favor. He began to shake and turned away from the couple, not wanting to be recognized by the killer he'd been hunting for several years. He wouldn't pick a public place to confront the ex-priest. He was no longer a cop; he was a private citizen in a foreign country. The detective was well informed on where to find Billy, and he would do so when prepared to do the inevitable. There was no thought of extradition or appeal to the local police. He had to kill the man who had snuffed out the life of his two partners and thirteen others.

Several hours passed before Billy and Nada started their journey back to the palace. As they approached the estate, Billy noticed it was in complete darkness.

It was foreboding and didn't feel right to the fugitive. He reached for his pistol from below his seat.

Nada feared possible evil or harm lay ahead. What she was about to witness would be a horrifying imprint, never to be erased.

Billy cautiously approached the entrance to the palace, with Nada close by his side. All lights were turned off, but he reached for the light switch and flipped it on. The scene was too much to bear, and Nada collapsed to the floor.

The prince and his wife had been beheaded and disemboweled. Their bodies were hanging by their feet, with pools of blood beneath. There was no sign of Tareq, and Billy was frantic, concerned that his life was taken by the assassins. He revived Nada, but she continued to tremble from the horrific scene. They searched for her nephew, approaching his bedroom with consternation.

When they opened the door, the scene was overwhelming. Billy fell to his knees, and Nada wailed, her body rocking from side-to-side. The young prince had suffered the same fate as his parents—beheaded and disemboweled. It devastated Billy; he had become a surrogate parent to the young prince and he failed to protect him. He lowered the boy's body and buried him with his parents.

Nada beseeched Billy to leave the palace and flee to safety.

"The palace is the best place for refuge until the morning," he explained to the woman. "The invaders have completed their murderous deed and have pillaged the palace. They won't return tonight."

They retreated to the bedroom, washing the bloodstains from their bodies before retiring, where Billy kept a gun at his side.

The next morning, Billy outlined his escape plan to Nada—they would board a ship leaving from Tripoli and bound for Turkey. They had to leave within the hour in order to safely meet the time constraints for the departure of the steamer. They would leave with just the clothing they were wearing—"We can purchase what we need along the way"—said Billy, Nada, taking a small case of incidentals. They left the bedroom and were proceeding toward the exit of the palace when a man stepped from the shadows to block their path. Billy pulled his gun from the holster; the man moved behind a large column.

"Who are you, and what do you want!" Billy shouted.

"You have to pay for the people you've murdered, Billy."

Although he was spooked, Billy said, "I don't know you. Just leave before you die."

"Yes, you do know me, Father Billy John Pratt. You killed two of my partners, and now it's time to pay."

"Is that you, Detective Kelly?"

"Yes, it is … and I'm your worst nightmare, Billy."

"Kelly, you have no jurisdiction here and no extradition agreement with the United States, so you go to hell."

"First you, killer. That's why I'm here—to guarantee your passage. You can be sure how this is going to end."

"Yes, you're going to join the partners I had the pleasure of killing. They never saw it coming, but you will, Kelly." Billy fired a shot that ricocheted off the marble stanchion.

"There's no way out, killer—not alive."

"That's where you're wrong, Kelly." The ex-priest stepped from the shadows, holding a gun to Nada's head. "Do you have it in you to kill this woman to get to me? If so, go ahead and shoot; if not, get out of my way. I'm leaving this hellhole, and you're a dead man if you try to stop me. But first, I'll blow this pretty woman's head off. You want her death on your hands?"

Before Kelly could respond, shots were fired from the front of the palace, placing all of their lives in danger. The revolutionaries had returned to plunder the remains of the palace.

"Now you've done it, you dumb bastard," Billy shouted. "These guys take no prisoners. They've just beheaded the prince, his wife, and their son. Either we figure out how to work together, or they'll chop us to pieces. Your call, Kelly."

The militia advanced, firing their guns in the direction of the men—hated rivals who now were faced with collaboration or certain annihilation.

"I'm coming in your direction, Billy. Cover my back," Kelly said.

The ex-priest fired a round in the Boston cop's direction, killing one of the advancing assassins.

"I saved your life, Detective. You owe me."

"That doesn't change a thing, killer," declared the cop from Boston.

The gunfire continued. Both men covered a targeted area and determined the number of marauders was limited to five. They reasoned if they killed one or two of the remaining intruders, the others would cut and run. Their ammunition was limited and they had to make every round count, so they held their fire until an open target appeared.

One of the men shouted out in Arabic, and Billy asked Nada for the translation.

"So she is with you. I thought I recognized her from the hotel restaurant," Kelly barked.

"Yes, she is, and she's very valuable if we want to survive this."

"The man claims to be part of the new ruling government," Nada translated. "He's telling us to surrender and we'll be given mercy."

"Tell him to drop their weapons, and we'll leave without further shooting," Billy ordered.

When Nada relayed the message, gunfire from the rebels sprayed the column the three were using for cover. They didn't return fire; they had to conserve their remaining bullets.

Kelly suggested a way to end the stalemate. He was concerned that the renegades would call for reinforcements and overwhelm their position. It was risky, but the alternative was unacceptable. He explained the plan to Billy and Nada. The young woman lowered her head, embarrassed by the proposition, but she reluctantly agreed.

Nada began speaking in Arabic to the insurgents, revealing that she wasn't with the men they sought. She said she was a prisoner, forced to perform unspeakable acts, and she would do the same for them if they would let her captors pass. She then emerged from behind the column, naked, her arms in the air. Two rebels exposed themselves to a line of fire; both were killed by Kelly and the ex-priest, as Nada retreated for cover. The remaining two insurgents ran off, clearing the way for Billy, Kelly, and Nada.

Kelly pointed his gun at Billy, demanding that he turn and face his executioner.

"I saved your life, Detective. You owe me. I could have let that guy kill you on the spot."

"But you took fifteen other lives, Billy. It's time to meet your Maker, and may he condemn your soul to burn in hell."

Those were the last words spoken by the former Boston detective. Nada swung a club to the head of the would-be-slayer of her man. Kelly's gun discharged when his body struck the floor, the bullet hitting the ex-priest in the lower torso. Nada screamed, but assisted Billy to their car. He was bleeding, but the bullet had cleanly exited his body. She ripped part of her tunic, stuffing the wound, and securing the bandage with another part of her robe.

Billy remained conscious and encouraged Nada to go back and kill the man who had shot him. She spurned the idea, telling him they had to flee the palace before more insurgents appeared. They headed to Tripoli, hoping the steamer they were to board for Turkey was still in port.

Kelly regained consciousness and commandeered the insurgents' jeep. He was frustrated and disappointed that he had let his guard down. He was too close to resolving his hunt-and-destroy mission, and the former detective was determined to find the killer and finish the job.

Suddenly, shots rang out. The two fleeing insurgents wanted their hijacked jeep, as it was their only means out of the palace. They obviously had called for reinforcements—that seemed the only reason for them to remain at the palace.

Bullets penetrated the vehicle in which Kelly was attempting to make his getaway. One grazed his shoulder and the fuel line of the jeep. Kelly ignored the pain. He was more concerned with reaching his destination before his fuel was depleted.

When Nada and Billy arrived in Tripoli, the steamer was still in port. They boarded the ship and paid the captain in cash. He directed one of his men to escort the passengers to their quarters, but explained to his travelers that repairs on the vessel still were not complete. The ship, however, would be departing for Turkey within the hour. At Nada's request, the captain sent the ship's medical officer to Billy's cabin. He sterilized his wound and replaced the makeshift dressing. He then injected an antibiotic directly to the injury. The long, thin needle penetrated the skin, causing a grimace from the man on the run. The medic dispensed Percocet to ease Billy's pain.

Twenty-five minutes from Tripoli, Kelly was racing to the port. He calculated that Billy had made arrangements to leave the country, and the only immediate way out was by sea, as airports and rails had been closed by the revolutionary insurgents. He looked to the heavens, appealing to a higher judge and praying that he wasn't too late to invoke the penalty on a man he considered pure evil. It was a conundrum for the Catholic detective, his requesting God to sanction the killing of another, but the boundaries of civility were abandoned, and the murder of his partners was his defense. His foot pressed down on the accelerator, and he rushed to deliver the punishment he had imagined for so many years.

The ship's horns blasted the silence of the evening, and the vessel's lines were released from the dock. The ship would take four or five days to reach its destination in Turkey, depending upon the weather.

Nada knew very little about the man she consorted with in betraying her

Muslim traditions. While he lay in bed, she asked about his boyhood, where he grew up and his childhood experiences.

He explained that he was raised in a poor section of Pittsburgh, that his father worked for the railroad, and his mother was a seamstress. He said his dad was a heavy drinker and usually stopped at the local tavern before coming home. His father was an abusive drunk, often arguing with his mother and sometimes getting physical. When he thought Billy was disrespectful, the large belt around his waist was put to use.

"We were a Catholic family, attending church on Sundays and the religious days of obligation. If someone had looked at our family, they would have assumed only good things. But the devil was in the details, and when my father went on a rampage, I would hide in the closet of my room, crying until he left the house or fell asleep wherever he left the bottle. The next payday, it was like déjà vu. At times, I wanted to run away as far as my imagination would allow. But it never got better until my mother had enough. The next time he laid his hands on her, she took a steak knife and planted it on his throat, screaming, 'You no good Irish bastard! If you ever touch me or the boy again, I swear to the Almighty, John Pratt, the last thing you'll hear is this knife cutting your miserable throat. Now, so we're clear in what I'm saying, blink those fucking eyes twice—twice, I say, for me and the boy!' It was the first time I had ever heard my mother use a bad word. Obviously, my father saw the devil in my mother's eyes and swore before the cross he'd never drink again.

"I wasn't into sports, but I played the games every nine- or ten year old does. My trouble began when I was twelve; it shaped who I became and what I wanted. When I look back in time, I can't conceive the Jekyll-and-Hyde I became. It was problematic, I guess, when you consider the evil side of life that I chose to swim in; it was pure debauchery. I'm going to need a couple of those painkillers, Nada."

She placed two pills in his mouth and provided water to swallow them down.

"I hope I'm not boring you with the story of my life," Billy said.

"No, you're not, but I do have a question, and I hope you don't object to my asking?"

"Fire away, Nada."

"How did you feel when you killed for the first time?"

Billy found it strange she would pursue the sensitive topic, and he hesitated to answer. "I found it thrilling, Nada. If the truth be told, to hold the last breath of a person's life in your hands is the most intoxicating feeling in the world. It becomes addictive after your first victim; thereafter, it's like a drug. You want more to satisfy the rush," he confessed.

The Muslim woman now challenged her steadfast loyalty to the heinous side of the man. "What about the family and the pregnant woman you left behind?"

"I see Prince Abdul was whispering in your ear. Nada, when you're a man on the run, every contingency must be taken into account. You must be disciplined and committed to abandon everything at a moment's notice, even those you care about. People are tools, and once they become an impediment, it's time to cast them aside," said the killer of fifteen. The Percocet was loosening his tongue, and he revealed more than he had intended.

Nada now realized that she too was a so-called tool and would be abandoned, if and when her lover was threatened. She heard the dark side of the ex-priest, and her trust and loyalty became a cavity of fear and survival. She no longer felt safe; a foreboding alarm had been triggered.

Billy fell asleep, and Nada went to the front deck of the ship, where the sea mist sprayed her body.

A voice from behind her interrupted her thoughts of plans to flee when they reached Turkey.

"Nada, I was startled when I woke and didn't see you at my side," Billy said, seeing the fear in her body language. "What's wrong? You seem worried." Billy realized he perhaps had confided too much information about his past.

"Don't turn around, Billy," said another voice. "Young lady, for your own safety, please move away from that piece of garbage." Kelly had boarded the only ship in port and paid the captain more than double what the killer had paid.

Billy whispered to Nada, demanding that she drop to her knees so he could turn and fire the gun in his waistband. There was a moment of eerie silence, and time seemed to have been suspended. Then, two shots rang out. Nada slowly rose, her face splattered with blood.

Billy fell backward, his life flashing in slices of time. Sequences of the past continued, as his body drifted toward the deck of the ship. His father using a strap to make his point. The molestation that defined his future. The faces of those he executed, waiting for atonement. The family he never cultivated. The last chance of redemption, lost for eternity.

He was thrown a curve by his own admissions. Now, the devil's ambassadors hovered, their talons ready. The killer's expression was one of terror. His final epitaph was his lifeless body, tumbling to the ship's deck.

Kelly reached for the pistol in Nada's trembling hand. He removed his jacket and placed it around her shoulders and gently removed the blood from her face with the bandana from his neck. He reached for his cell phone and took a series of photos of the killer from Boston. Then he tossed Billy's body into the sea. Thus, the chase that had spanned four continents came to a close.

When Kelly returned to Boston, he presented the photo evidence to his former commander, who was astonished that the detective had survived his search for the killer.

The captain reached into a drawer and placed Mike's badge and gun on his desk.

Mike hesitated. The man who had brought closure to the victims' families, placed his hand on the items that identified his career and pushed them back to his former commander.

"What will you do, Mike? You know the job is in your blood."

"I'll explore my options, Captain," Kelly responded.

The story of the killing of the infamous murderer was the headline in the media, and demand for Kelly's story commanded interest from talk shows, publishers, and Hollywood.

Two years later, *The Tattered Collar* was on the *New York Times* best-seller list for six weeks, and a movie of Billy's exploits was in production.

Printed in the United States
By Bookmasters